Books by Anina Collins

THE FINEST HOUR

ANINA COLLINS

The Finest Hour

Join Poppy and Alex for the final Poppy McGuire mystery!

For three years, Poppy and Alex have worked together solving cases in their small town of Sunset Ridge, first as just co-workers but later as partners in nearly every sense of the word. Now they're about to take the final step and become husband and wife, but in the midst of getting ready for what folks around town are calling the wedding of the year, the murder of someone involved in the preparations makes their plans go awry.

Samuel Morrow, the kind man who has run Morrow's Jewelers for over twenty years, is found murdered in an apparent break-in, and there's no shortage of suspects who may have had a reason to kill him. Oddly enough, something very valuable to Poppy and Alex is missing from his store too. Is the theft connected to the murder?

As they hunt for Samuel's killer, carefully eliminating suspect after suspect, they must juggle cake tastings and reception planning, as all the while someone's watching their favorite amateur sleuth. Will Poppy and Alex solve the case and reach the altar, or will the killer make their ever after far less than happy?

Chapter One

THREE MONTHS OF searching for a maid of honor dress may have been a new world's record. At least it felt like it could be. Holly, my good friend from college who had the honor or torture of being my maid of honor, depending on how you looked at it, had given the thumbs down to every dress we'd seen since we started this quest one snowy day in February.

We'd searched the three biggest dress shops in Baltimore and one in Frederick, and all with no success. Now we found ourselves back in the dressing room at Michelle's Dress Shop in Sunset Ridge, the place we'd started in the first place, and still no luck.

Each time it was a variation on the same theme. The blue dress had too much frilliness to it. The green one hugged her body too closely and showed off her slightly imperfect figure. And I mean very slightly. Holly Richardson ran every day and took great care of herself, and her body showed it. But no matter what she did, her hips were always just a little too big for her liking.

I thought she looked incredible in everything she wore, including every bridesmaid dress she tried on. That fact aside, I understood her pickiness. I just wished that magical dress she'd love would come along soon.

These Saturday treks around Maryland to search for it were killing me.

Holly stood on the pink carpeted dais and stared at herself in the triple mirror as she tugged at the light blue dress that made her pretty face twist into a look of disgust. Even that didn't ruin the very cute thing she had going on with her short black hair and stunning green eyes.

At least in my opinion.

Not that I liked the dress that much. With its puffy sleeves and wide bottom, it reminded me of something the Founders Day Planning Committee would want every woman in town to wear for one of their historical celebrations.

"It's so poofy, Poppy. You don't really want me to wear this in your wedding, do you?" Holly asked with fear in her voice.

I shook my head. "No, it's not right. I think we need to move on to the next one. Michelle brought in another dress that might work. I hadn't planned on a black and white wedding, but it could work."

Holly trudged back toward the dressing area to change out of the light blue poofy dress, so I grabbed the sleek black number off the rack and took it to her. Sticking my hand in through the curtain, I said, "It's definitely not like the other one. Maybe this will work."

She took the hanger from me. "I'm sorry I'm so difficult about this, Poppy. I just want it to be perfect. How is it possible that bridesmaid's dresses are all so ugly? Even the ones in Baltimore weren't right. Is this some kind of conspiracy to make all bridesmaids hideous?"

Her comment made me chuckle, even though I

knew the frustration in her voice was genuine. "I think I heard at some point that the dresses ensured that the bride is always the most beautiful woman in the room. That's why you can't wear white to a wedding, I think."

I heard her grunt and groan as she pulled the dress over her body. "What does it matter what anyone else looks like at the wedding? Alex is only going to be looking at you anyway. I think these rules were made up by insecure women who knew they were marrying dogs who would be cheating on them not a few months into the marriage."

Her lack of romanticism lately could be traced directly to the breakup of her own marriage a few months ago. Her soon-to-be ex-husband Chase, whose name now seemed more prophetic than anyone could imagine when they first got together, had cheated on her with at least three women that she knew of, and that didn't include all the women she suspected him of cheating with.

She had every right to be sour on romance. I knew I would be. I had been for years after Jared ran off with that Food King check-out girl.

"What's it look like? Come out and let me see," I asked, hoping this would be the dress that would finally put an end to our quest.

Holly pushed the curtain off to the side and shook her head. "Nope. Not this one either."

I scanned the dress from the thin straps that came over her shoulders to the fitted bodice that hugged her body beautifully. Confused, I asked, "Why? It's gorgeous. If it's the black thing, that's okay. I know we aren't having an evening wedding, but I don't think anyone will care if we break this wedding rule. I know I won't, and trust me, Alex won't care."

Holding one finger up, she smirked. "One moment. You haven't seen the whole thing."

And then she slowly spun around to show me the back, and I instantly saw the problem with this dress.

She shook her behind, which stuck nearly halfway out of the dress, and looked back at me. "You still like it? Talk about people paying attention to the wrong thing at your wedding! As you two recite your vows, all anyone will be looking at is me mooning the entire congregation," she said with a laugh.

Definitely not the right dress.

"Okay, that's a big no. Let me go ask Michelle if she has anything else that would cover your entire butt. For what it's worth, I like the front a lot, if that's any consolation."

Holly walked back into the dressing room and pulled the curtain closed as she yelled out, "As long as I'm not mooning people. That's a hard line I won't cross. I may be single again, but even that doesn't mean I want my butt cheeks hanging out for all the world to see."

After finding Michelle out at the register, I explained about the air conditioned backside of the most recent dress and asked her if she had something similar to the way that dress looked just with more fabric on the rear. She thought for a moment and then handed me a pale yellow dress I immediately checked to make sure Holly wouldn't be mooning anyone if she wore it. Satisfied it would cover all her body parts that legally should be covered, I headed back to the dressing area.

I had a feeling Holly wouldn't be crazy about the pale yellow color with her black hair, but desperate times called for desperate measures. The wedding was only three weeks away, and if we didn't find a dress that day, I didn't know what we'd do.

"Michelle swears all your bits and pieces will be covered with this one, so let's see how it goes," I said cheerily, hoping my upbeat attitude would make her want to look past the color.

"Yellow?" she asked in horror as she took the hanger and dress from my hold. "So the bumblebee look is what you're going for?"

"It's not that kind of yellow. Just try it on and maybe if it looks good, we can ask Michelle if there's a way we can rush order a different color in the same dress."

I sat down on the pink upholstered chair that almost matched the color of the carpet covering the dais in front of the mirrors and waited to see how she looked in the newest last chance dress. A minute later, she appeared and I knew this dress wouldn't work either.

"The look on your face tells me what I thought when I first saw it was right," Holly said as she sat down on the dais defeated. "I'm going to be the ugliest bridesmaid in history, Poppy. You know, there's still time for you to pick someone else."

Hoping to cheer her up, I stood from the chair and said, "Hang on. Maybe if I show you my dress that will help us choose something right."

My friend hung her head and sighed. "I don't think it could hurt."

I retrieved my wedding gown from Michelle and headed back into the dressing room to get into it. The white dress fit perfectly, and as I looked in the mirror at myself, I felt more beautiful than ever before in all my life.

Pulling back the curtain, I stepped out into the

dressing area and heard Holly gasp when she looked at me in it for the first time. That's what the perfect dress was supposed to do. I only hoped Alex would have the same response when he saw me walking down the aisle.

She stood up and walked over to me, her mouth hanging open. "Oh my God, Poppy. It's gorgeous. I'm speechless. Alex is going to lose his mind when he sees you in this dress."

I looked down at my wedding gown in tears at the idea that it would do that. "I know it's simple and doesn't have a lot going on with it, but I liked it."

Turning around, I showed off my favorite part of the dress. "Look at the bow in the back. I thought that was so cute when I saw it."

"I love how it's basically backless, except for the sheer fabric on each side of the V in the back. You look so incredible in this, Poppy. I mean it. Alex is going to lose his mind at how stunning you look. It's perfect for you."

I stepped up onto the dais and looked at myself in the three mirrors in front of me. "I love the lace on the bottom of the dress too. It comes out from my waist and looks so delicate."

Holly stood behind me and smiled. "It's the only dress I can imagine you getting married in. It's a combination of wholesome and slightly sexy that's quintessentially you, Poppy."

Looking back at her, I asked, "Does it help you with what kind of dress you might want to wear, though?"

She nodded and stepped off the dais. "I think so. Give me a couple minutes. I'm going to ask Michelle if she has something that just popped into my head. Don't take your dress off yet, though. I want to see the two of us standing together."

Holly returned a few minutes later with a pale pink dress that resembled the black dress from earlier. Before I could say anything about the back of it, she assured me there would be none of her hanging out in this one and hurried into the dressing room.

"I think this is the one, Poppy," she called out as she slipped into it.

"Really?" I asked, truly hoping she was right.

"Your idea of showing me your dress was a great one. I wish you would have mentioned it months ago," she joked.

"Me too," I said with a chuckle.

A few seconds later, she stepped out into the dressing area and I knew she was right. The pale pink dress hung close to her body but looked perfect on her from the spaghetti straps on her shoulders to where it slightly pooled at her feet. The color worked just right with her dark hair and olive skin, and I wondered how we'd missed this dress for so long.

She took her place next to me in front of the triple mirrors and smiled at me. "Isn't it perfect?"

Nodding, I sighed with relief. "It's perfect. Our quest is complete. And it's not even going to take too much in alterations to make it fit. Just a little off the bottom once you put shoes on."

"So now that we finally found a dress, what else do you have to do with wedding prep?" Holly asked, bringing the reality of the next few weeks crashing into my brain.

I thought about all the things that had yet to be done for our perfect today to be just that. Alex and I still had to choose the menu for the reception, attend the cake tasting, which was scheduled for two days later on Monday, and we had to decide where to go on their honeymoon.

Just thinking about all of that made my stomach twist into knots.

"At least the rings are taken care of. We had them specially made at a jeweler in town who's the best at unique pieces. You should see them. Alex's is a simple gold band with an inscription inside, and mine is a gold band with diamonds and an inscription inside."

Holly smiled wickedly and asked, "What do the inscriptions say?"

I shook my head. "It's private between us, but they say what's in our hearts."

"Ooooh, I love it! So romantic! I wish I believed in romance like that anymore."

Wrapping my arms around her shoulders, I squeezed her to me. "You will. Just give it a little time. Chase was just one guy, one fish in a big ocean. Don't give up. Trust me. There are good people like you out there."

Just then, I heard my phone ringing in my purse over on the chair and recognized it as Alex's ringtone. "Speaking of good, there's my knight in shining armor now. Hang on."

I hopped off the dais and rummaged through my purse to answer the phone. "Hey you! What's new?"

"Poppy, we've got a case. Want me to head out alone or are you guys done at the bridal shop?"

Suddenly, I felt torn between going to work on a case and hanging out with Holly, but she saw my hesitation and said, "Go. I have to get Michelle to alter this dress so I can walk down the aisle without falling on my face. I'll call you later."

"Alex, I'll meet you there."

"I haven't told you what the case is yet," he said in serious voice.

I laughed and walked to the dressing room to get changed into my street clothes. "Oh yeah. So what's the case about?"

"Samuel Morrow was found dead in his jewelry shop a few minutes ago. Craig's there and thinks it might be a robbery gone sideways. How soon can you get there?"

His words hit me like a ton of bricks, and suddenly, my body felt like I didn't have the strength to stand. I leaned against the dressing room wall and took a deep breath in as what he said sunk in.

"Samuel Morrow? Oh, my God, Alex. We were just in his store a week ago. I just saw him the other day and waved at him as I walked to the station."

"I know. He was one of the good guys. I'm heading to his store now. If you don't want to work on this, that's okay. I know you have other things going on this morning."

For the first time, I wasn't sure I wanted to work on a case with Alex. I sat down and my body sagged. "I don't know. Maybe I'll sit this one out."

"It's okay, Poppy. I'll give you a call and see if you're around for lunch in a few hours. Love you."

"I love you too. Talk to you later."

I ended the call and let the phone drop onto the lap of my wedding dress. I'd always loved investigating cases with Alex, but this one at this time felt too close to home. Samuel Morrow, the man who we'd spent hours with designing our wedding rings, murdered. Who would want to kill him?

"Everything okay in there, Poppy?" Holly said on the other side of the dressing room curtain.

"Yeah. Just a case that Alex called me about. I'll be out in a few minutes."

"Okay. I'm going to start working with Michelle on the alterations of my dress and then I have to run back to the office. I'll call you later, okay?"

"I'll talk to you later, Holly."

I heard her walk out into the shop and let a deep sigh leave my body. How could anyone hurt Samuel Morrow?

And why?

As I WALKED toward my house on Barn Street, I couldn't stop thinking of Samuel Morrow and how wonderful he'd been when Alex and I worked with him on our rings. Who would want to kill him?

My phone rang, tearing me from my thoughts, and I looked to see it was Alex.

"Poppy, I'd like you to come to Samuel Morrow's shop. Right now."

I heard something strange in his voice. What was wrong with Alex? He'd never been so insistent before.

"When did you get so demanding?" I asked, wondering if this was how he was going to be now that we were going to be married. "I told you I didn't want to work this case."

"Please come here right now. Okay?" he said, clearly upset about something.

"What's going on, Alex? Why are you acting like this?"

"I don't want to argue about this, Poppy. I just need you to come to the jewelry shop. Right now," Alex said quietly, his tone frightening me.

Chapter Two

S AMUEL MORROW'S JEWELRY shop was located three blocks up Main Street from the police station in a section of the street many Sunset Ridge citizens referred to as the business district. As far as business districts went, it wasn't much, but along with his jewelry store, there was French's Hardware Store, Martin's Pharmacy, and Cardow's Shoe Store. Not exactly even strip mall level, but for a small town, it wasn't too bad.

There had been more when I was a little girl, but big box stores and the mall in Frederick had cut into local business and caused many of them to close. But most people in Sunset Ridge believed in keeping the town's remaining stores open and vibrant, so unlike many small town businesses, these four shops were often quite busy.

I hurried past the shoe store and saw Nate Cardow inside helping a young mother and her two little boys who were seated in front of him. Well, the mother sat. Her two sons bounced in their seats and wiggled their legs as Nate struggled to fit the smaller boy's feet into a pair of shoes. The scene was at once humorous and frustrating to watch, but no matter how much the child squirmed, Nate patiently worked to get his little foot into that shoe.

Yellow police crime scene tape blocked the entrance to Morrow's Jewelry Shop, forcing me to duck underneath it, and I walked into the store as I had any other murder scene I'd been at. After nearly a dozen, I could say I was used to them, as much as anyone could be accustomed to seeing the place where someone lost their life.

Behind the glass cases that faced the front door, Alex and Craig stood conducting their initial investigation. Craig wrote feverishly in a small notebook he'd begun carrying after he started working with Alex, in an effort to emulate the man who'd become a mentor to him, while Alex stood with his arms folded staring down at the floor where I suspected Samuel Morrow lay. The coroner stood off to the side with his two assistants talking in a low voice and pointing at where Alex stared.

Although the scene resembled nearly every other one I'd been at, suddenly my legs felt weak, like at any moment they'd give out and I'd crumble to the floor in a heap of unsupported bones and flesh. Hoping to steady myself, I grabbed a hold of the glass display case next to me before announcing my arrival as casually as possible.

"Hey, guys!" I said in my usual cheery voice, forced at the moment.

Alex took one look at me and rushed over to my side as everyone else simply smiled and said hello as they always did. My fiancé knew me too well, though, and sensed something was wrong as I stood there with a smile pasted on my face.

Just before he reached me, I caught a glimpse of Samuel Morrow lying on the floor behind the jewelry case in a pool of his own blood with shattered glass surrounding his body. My gaze focused on the bullet hole in the middle of his forehead and then immediately on his steel grey hair he always took such care to meticulously keep slicked back and stylish but now looked unkempt, especially around his temples where the hair stuck out straight from his head.

The effect made his demise all the more real because I knew Samuel Morrow would never let himself be seen like that if he had a choice. But someone had taken that choice from him, violently and mercilessly.

"Poppy, is everything okay?" Alex asked as he reached me.

All at once, my stomach roiled at the sight of Samuel Morrow lying there dead, and I covered my mouth with my hand, afraid I might vomit at any moment.

Quickly, Alex wrapped his arms around me and escorted me to a storeroom off the main storefront. Shaking my head, I tried to dispel what I'd seen just a moment before, but that vision wouldn't leave my mind. I wasn't sure it ever would.

"What's wrong, Poppy?" he asked, obviously confused by my reaction.

Why wouldn't he be? I'd seen dead bodies before on cases we worked together, so why would he think this one would bother me?

I shook my head faster in an effort to push all the bad out of my mind. It didn't work.

"I don't know. Just seeing Samuel on the floor like that got to me. Did you see his hair? He'd never let it be like that if he could."

Alex nodded. "I know," he said in his deep voice that made me feel safe and secure.

As much as I didn't want to cry, the tears welled up in my eyes and before I knew it, I was standing there in

Samuel Morrow's dusty storeroom sobbing. Alex pulled me close so my face pressed against his chest, and for a long minute, I just cried.

I didn't know why. Well, other than a person I knew and liked lay dead just a few yards away from me, I didn't know why I was crying. Part of me felt foolish and stupid, but another part of me didn't know any other way to express my sadness at Samuel's death.

"I'm sorry, Poppy, but I wanted you here with me."

The way he said that made me feel needed but also didn't make any sense. I looked up at him, confused. Alex had never needed me to work on a case. Even I knew that.

"Why? What do I bring to this case, other than knowing Samuel, which everyone else in town can claim?"

Alex hesitated, drawing his black eyebrows in like slashes that made him look more worried than I'd seen him in months. I waited to hear his answer, and finally, he said, "This looks like a robbery that turned bad. Something was taken. Something having to do with us."

"Us? What do you mean?" I asked as my mind raced to the only items in the store that had to do with us.

Our wedding bands.

But why would anyone want to steal our wedding bands?

"Oh my God! Someone stole our wedding rings? Who would do that?" I asked as my mind whirled from the mere idea.

Alex held me by my shoulders and explained in that calm voice I'd heard him use with victim's families, "Poppy, they took just one of our rings."

"What? What do you mean?"

"They only took yours."

I stared up into his dark eyes and saw real concern in them that worried me even more. "Just mine? Why would anyone take just my ring?"

Slowly shaking his head, he said, "I don't know, but until this case is solved, I want you by my side. Something feels very wrong here. I don't think this was a coincidence."

Grabbing onto his black uniform shirt, I clutched it in my hand as everything around me seemed to give way. "What do you mean you don't think this was a coincidence? What if the person thought they were about to get caught and ran out in a hurry? Maybe they'd only get to take one thing and my ring happened to be it."

No matter how panicked I was quickly becoming, the rational side of my brain told me this sounded unlikely. But why would anyone just want my ring? Then the worst truth of all this dawned on me.

Samuel was murdered over my ring. My ring.

Barely able to hold back the tears, I asked, "Alex, did someone kill poor Samuel Morrow because of my wedding band? Oh, my God. I'm going to be sick. Why would anyone do that for a ring?"

I buried my head in his chest again and reveled in the feel of his arms holding me as I sobbed over the death of such a sweet man. Alex hugged me to him and whispered, "We don't know all the facts yet. We don't know what happened. I just want you next to me from now on until we get this case solved, okay?"

I looked up at him and dried my eyes. "What is going on? Why are you worried about this?"

"I don't know. I just don't want to take any chances,

so don't fight me on this. I know you didn't want to work this case, but I want you nearby. Just to be safe."

"Safe from what, Alex? What would I have to be safe from?" I asked, still confused.

Alex pulled me into the back of the store away from Craig and whispered, "Out of an entire jewelry store, someone decided to take just your wedding ring? That doesn't sound strange to you? Maybe it's just a coincidence, but I don't want to take any chances."

The thought that someone did this all to take my ring sounded insane, but I saw in Alex's expression he was truly worried. I took a deep breath and wiped the last tears from under my eyes before forcing a smile.

"Okay. I'll stick like glue to you. How's that?"

Alex smiled and kissed me on the forehead. "Good. I can't let anything happen to my bride, after all. Without you, this whole marriage thing doesn't happen. You're an integral part of it."

"Well, it's good to know I'm important in this world," I said as he turned to head back to the front of the store.

We walked out to where Craig stood looking down at Donny as he completed his preliminary examination. The coroner looked up from Samuel's body when he heard us walk around the counter and smiled up at me.

"It's getting close to the big day. You two ready?"

Steeling myself, I smiled and nodded. "Ready as we're ever going to be. Did you send in your RSVP for the reception, Donny? I don't think I remember seeing your name in the confirmed column."

The coroner stood up and smacked himself in his extraordinarily large forehead. "I knew I'd forget. That's why I told you I'd be there right after you invited me."

"Thankfully, I remembered, but I need to know who your plus one is."

Everyone around us stopped what they were doing and stared at Donny to hear who he planned to bring to the wedding reception. The Sunset Ridge coroner was notoriously secretive about his personal life, although Derek had commented more than once that he assumed all Donny did when he wasn't dealing with dead bodies was read books about them.

To be honest, I had a hard time imagining him with a woman only because the man seemed to wear the same five or six shirts all the time, even though a couple of them had obvious stains no amount of washing could remove. If he had a woman in his life, that wouldn't happen. No woman would allow a man she cared about to walk around like that.

Noticing everyone looking at him, he grimaced and rolled his eyes before grumbling, "Just assume I'm coming alone. No need to show any of you guys who I spend my hours off with."

One of his assistants from the coroner's office laughed and said, "Planning on bringing your big screen TV and a six pack of beer with you to the reception, Donny?"

Donny shot him a nasty look and snapped, "Just get that body in the wagon and stop flapping your gums."

Alex looked at me and gave me a tiny smile before turning back to pay attention to Donny. "Any ideas on what killed him?"

"I'm going with the obvious for now and saying a gunshot to the head. If I find anything else that would make more sense, I'll let you know. In the meantime, let's go with this being a shooting. I'm guessing early this morning, if that helps at all. Right around dawn, say between six and seven am."

He turned on his heels and walked out past his assistant, throwing him a glare. After they left, I nudged Alex in the side and whispered, "I feel wrong joking around with poor Samuel lying there dead."

"I know, but it's just how we handle this job."

"I know. I know. I'm just overly emotional today," I said, shaking my head. "I need to get into the game. Anything else I missed?"

"I don't think so."

"So far, then, Samuel is dead from a gunshot wound to the head and only one item was stolen in a jewelry store full of expensive pieces. And that one item had no real worth, except to the two of us."

Alex said nothing but nodded. I knew the fact that Samuel may have died because of my ring bothered him. I just wished it didn't make me want to cry for the third time that day.

Craig cleared his throat, and the two of us turned to face him as Donny's men wheeled Samuel out on their stretcher. "The state police forensics lab is here to do their work on fingerprints. Anything I should tell them?"

"No," Alex said, shaking his head. "Just stay until they're done and make sure the scene is contained before you leave. I'm going to speak to Samuel's wife and break the news to her. Meet us back at the station when you're done."

"Will do."

Two forensics officers walked in and gave us a silent nod as we left to go to Samuel's home and speak to his wife, Eliza. Of all the times I'd accompanied Alex on this part of the job, this one would be the most difficult of all.

I'd never met Samuel's wife, but I knew from the way he spoke of her that she was the love of his life.

I could only imagine she felt the same and would be devastated by the news Alex had to give her.

Settling into the passenger seat of the police cruiser beside him, I took a deep breath and let it out slowly. What had been a wonderful day with Holly finally finding a dress the two of us loved had turned into one of the worst days in recent memory.

Alex reached over and wove his fingers through mine for a moment before gently squeezing my hand in his. "If you want, you can wait in the car while I speak to Samuel's wife."

As much as I wanted to take him up on that offer, I wanted to be strong more, so I shook my head. "No, I'll go with you. It will give me a chance to extend my sympathies. I remember how much that meant when my mother died."

His hand slid from mine, and he pulled away from the curb. We drove down Main Street toward Victorian Row and in a couple minutes we were parked in front of Samuel Morrow's very elegant slate blue and grey Victorian home. Not even half a mile from his shop, he'd walked to work every day since opening his store in 1992.

Little details like that were the kinds of things he liked to talk about when he spoke to customers. I'd always appreciated that since I knew he wasn't native to Sunset Ridge. Coming from New York, he could have been standoffish. My father had mentioned more than once that people viewed him as an outsider for the first year or so he lived in town, but once they got to know him, they didn't think of Samuel as a former New

Yorker or transplant to our small town.

He was just Samuel Morrow, the jeweler with a store on Main Street.

And now as Alex turned the car off and I looked out at Samuel's gorgeous home he so proudly showed off every holiday season with decorations that far surpassed everyone's in town, I prepared myself to listen to Alex tell his wife that he'd been murdered sometime early this morning.

The car door opened, and I looked up to see Alex holding his hand out. "You sure you want to do this? I can handle it on my own. It's okay, Poppy."

I took his hand and stepped out of the car onto the sidewalk. "I can do this."

We walked up the perfectly white concrete sidewalk to the grey painted stairs that matched the rest of the huge wrap around porch that made the house so elegant looking. Before we could ring the doorbell, a middle aged woman wearing a maid's uniform and her light hair in a bun opened the front door and stepped out to greet us.

"Can I help you?" she asked in a small voice.

Alex walked up the steps to meet her and said, "My name is Officer Alex Montero. This is my partner Poppy McGuire. We'd like to speak to Mrs. Morrow."

The woman looked down at me on the sidewalk for a moment and then back at Alex before shaking her head. "I'm sorry, but Mrs. Morrow is out to Washington D.C. for the day."

"Do you know when she's expected back?" Alex asked.

"I expect her back by dinnertime, Officer Montero."

"Well, can you please give me her cell phone

number? I need to speak to her," he said, slightly more insistently than before.

Once again, the maid shook her head. "She doesn't have it on her today, unfortunately. She forgot to charge it, so she left it at home. I know Mr. Morrow left for work early today, so perhaps he could help you. I'm sure he's at his store on Main Street."

I winced at her mention of Samuel doing what he'd done every day but Sunday for two decades without fail. Alex simply shook his head.

"Thank you. Please tell Mrs. Morrow I was here and will return later today."

The maid smiled and walked back into the house. Alex joined me on the sidewalk and looked back before he began to head toward the car.

"I don't think she knows about Samuel yet, Alex. If she does, she deserves an Oscar," I said once we reached the car.

He glanced back at the house one more time. "I don't think so either, and even though I wasn't looking at the wife as a suspect, my gut says this feels odd."

"It could be a coincidence that the very day her husband is murdered is the same one she decides to take a trip to D.C."

Alex turned to face me and arched one dark eyebrow. "That would be the second coincidence in this case. I'm not a fan of coincidences, you know."

"I do. But sometimes those things just happen."

He shrugged and opened my car door for me. "For now, that's what they'll have to be. I think I want Craig to find out about Mrs. Morrow. All I know is she was married to Samuel. Do you know anything more?"

"Only what the gossips have said in the past," I said

with a slight smile, knowing Alex would be interested in what the old ladies in town had whispered about Eliza Morrow.

"Do tell," he said as I took my place in the passenger seat beside him.

"What do you say to going to The Grounds and getting a coffee first? Today calls for more caffeine than I've had this morning."

Alex turned to look at me and smiled. "It's a deal. I buy the coffee and you give me the gossip."

Chapter Three

THE GROUNDS HAD a large group of late morning coffee drinkers waiting for service when we arrived, so I quickly snagged a table while Alex staked out his spot in the long line that snaked back to the front door. Saturdays were always busy at the coffee shop, so I expected to be sitting alone for a while, but just a minute later, Pam came toward the table with a coffee cup in each hand.

"I saw you guys come in and figured I'd get your usual for you," she said with a broad grin. "Let me tell Alex so he doesn't have to stand in that line."

As she hurried away, I spun the Styrofoam cups around and saw the telltale shorthand written in black marker on each that indicated which one was mine and which was Alex's. On the cup in my right hand was written FR 4C 4S, my French Roast with four creams and four sugars. On the other cup all she'd written was B for the black coffee Alex enjoyed.

I pushed his coffee to the other side of the table and looked up to see him and Pam coming back. The expression on his face seemed to be a mixture of relief and confusion.

She pointed toward the empty chair and in a

motherly tone said, "Sit, sit. I got you your usual, so there's no need to stand in line."

Unused to the special treatment, Alex looked over at me and quietly thanked her as he sat down. "That's very nice of you, Pam. Thanks."

"Yes, thank you, Pam. You've really got a line out the door this morning," I said with a smile.

She waved off the thanks, shaking her head. "It's nothing. I wanted to talk to you two anyway, so it's nothing. Now how are the wedding plans going? Is everything set?"

Pam focused her complete attention on me as I tried to come up with an answer that didn't give away how utterly unprepared we actually were for our wedding just about a month away from that moment. She didn't need to know that, though.

"Just about," I chirped in my most chipper voice. "You know how these things go. You do everything you thought you had to do and then a half dozen things crop up and you have to take care of them. But don't worry. It's going to be great."

She waved her hand as if to indicate she had complete confidence that our wedding would be everything she'd made it out to be in her mind. "Of course! I can't wait! Even Gerald is excited. He's going to wear his black suit, even though he might roast in it if the weather suddenly gets hot like it's wont to do in late May here. Gerald looks so good in a suit, but I can never get him to put it on, so this is a good reason for him to dress up. And I'm going to wear my green print dress I got last year for the Founder's Day dance. But listen to me talking all about what we're going to wear, mere guests, when the star of the show is you. Tell me all about your dress!"

Out of the corner of my eye, I saw Alex twist his expression into the grimace that came whenever someone in town stopped to talk to us about the wedding. What I considered neighborly interest he saw as intrusive, and in the past few weeks, more and more Sunset Ridge folks had done just what Pam was doing whenever we were out in public.

Knowing this, I politely begged off talking about my dress, even though I desperately wanted to brag about it, and used the old superstition of the groom not supposed to see the gown before the wedding to get out of the conversation.

I made my eyes wide and pointed at Alex. "I can't say much because the groom is right here, but I can say I went for white and it's gorgeous! Just wait until you see it!"

My ploy worked instantly, and the concern that he might know something that could jinx our wedding day stopped Pam cold. Worry settled into her features, and she nodded knowingly.

"Oh, I understand. I wouldn't want to do anything to ruin the big day for either of you. I just know you'll make a beautiful bride, Poppy. It's going to be such a wonderful day."

She turned to look at Alex, who at the moment appeared as comfortable as someone about to go in for a root canal. "And I know you're going to make a dashing groom too, Alex."

He forced a smile that barely made the corners of his mouth creep up. "I'm going to do my best. Poppy's the real focus of attention, though. It's all about the bride."

Pam beamed at me and nodded. "It sure is. I'm so

happy for you two. Okay, I better get back there or that girl will have the line out the door and down the block. I'll see you later!"

I watched her trot back to the counter and offer to help the next customer in line. Pam's enthusiasm mirrored what I'd experienced pretty much since the day the engagement announcement appeared in *The Eagle*'s society section. From that point on, anytime people saw me, there was a good chance they wanted to talk about the wedding, with some even calling it the wedding of the year.

That seemed a bit much, but there was no denying that our fellow Sunset Ridge citizens were happy about our impending nuptials. Alex, on the other hand, didn't seem nearly as happy with their constant need to talk about it with us.

I looked over at him and saw the unhappiness in his face. "Hey, what's wrong?"

Not that I didn't already know the answer to that question.

"Nothing," he answered, clearly a lie.

"I know you don't like when people do things like that, like Pam just did, but it's only them being happy for us. They don't mean any harm."

"I guess."

I took a sip of coffee and let it slide down my throat, hoping he'd continue the conversation, but that wasn't Alex's style. He definitely lived up to the description of a man of few words. I obviously was the polar opposite of that, so I continued the conversation, needing to make sure our fellow citizens' interest in our wedding wasn't ruining it for him.

"Is everything okay?" I asked, wishing above all else

that he would say yes.

But the scowl he wore whenever anyone came up to us lately told me the answer definitely would be something else.

"Yeah. I mean, I'm fine. It's nothing, Poppy," he said, diverting his gaze from mine and looking past me toward the front windows of the coffee shop.

"It doesn't sound like nothing, Alex. Talk to me. Or at least look at me."

He did as I wanted and focused on me across from him. "I'm just not used to an entire town full of people involved in my business. That's all."

The way he said that told me that wasn't a small thing to him and he'd added the that's all onto the end of his statement for my benefit.

"But this is how Sunset Ridge is, Alex. It's been like this since we began working together."

He winced. "I guess, but this feels different somehow."

"Are you unhappy?"

Alex reached across the table and took my hand in his, shaking his head. "No, not at all. Don't think that, Poppy. Never. I'm just used to having my private life, well, private. But as you say, this is Sunset Ridge."

Hearing he wasn't unhappy made me smile, but I wondered if this was all having an effect on him. This would be his second wedding, so I suspected he didn't put as much emphasis on the whole big day idea as I and everyone else around us did.

"I think most of this is because of me, to be honest," I admitted. "You're marrying the one woman everyone thought would be single forever. It's made me a local celebrity in some ways."

Alex rolled his eyes in disgust, just like he did whenever I mentioned what the locals had thought of me for so long. "You're the brightest, most beautiful woman in this town, and these yahoos tagged you with the Old Maid label. Sometimes I wonder where I'm living, Poppy."

Before I could swoon over how much I loved it when he said things like that, I saw my editor from *The Eagle* walking toward our table. Just as he reached us, Alex muttered in disgust, "Another county heard from."

Looking up at my boss, I pasted a smile on my face. "Hi, Howard. What's new?"

A large man with a bulbous head that reminded me of some cartoon character who'd unfortunately had someone attach an air pump to his head and inflated it until it was close to exploding, he always appeared on the verge of blowing up at whoever he spoke to. Almost completely bald, he had little tufts of hair just above his ears that made a ring around his head and made it look like a fleshy Saturn sitting atop his neck.

Howard looked over at Alex but didn't say a word to him before turning his head to face me. "The Samuel Morrow murder is going to be full page news this afternoon. Is there anything you can give me that will make it the best reporting it can be?"

Always the leader in charm, Howard seemed particularly crass today.

Out of the corner of my eye, I saw a look of utter contempt come over Alex's face. Wincing, I said, "It's an active investigation, Howard, so I don't think there's anything I can add to help the reporters at this point. I can say I knew Samuel Morrow and thought very highly of him. Everyone in town loved him."

Howard let out a grunt like a pig. "Ugh. That kind of tripe doesn't sell papers, Poppy. You know better than that. You need to get rid of that sappy side if you ever want to get a byline with *The Eagle*."

He stormed away to the counter to get his coffee, and I looked across the table to see Alex's eyebrows up in his forehead and a pained look on his face. Suddenly, I felt the need to say something overcome me.

"I guess you think he's a monster. He is, but…"

"But what, Poppy? You don't have to defend him. You're too good for that newspaper anyway."

"Not according to Howard. I don't think I'll ever get a chance to do anything more than what I do now. And he wonders why I try to be out investigating with you as often as I can."

Howard's visit made my stomach roil once again that morning. His disregard for the loss of another human life sickened me. As I fought the bile creeping up into my throat, Alex reached across the table and squeezed my hand.

"Hey, don't let him get to you."

Almost instinctively, I forced a smile. "I know. He's just a ridiculously insensitive man with suits that hang strangely on him because his weight keeps yo-yoing. That he's my boss and editor is just something I have to deal with."

Alex smiled at my description of Howard. "Yeah, what is going with those suits of his? Last month, he looked like a ten pound sausage stuffed into a five pound casing in one of them I saw him in at the grocery store, and today he's swimming in his clothes."

I chuckled at his folksy description of Howard in his chubby period last month. "He's been doing some lemon juice and maple syrup diet, but as soon as he stops it, he binges on food and blows up again. At this point, I don't know who to expect on any given day I have to see him, skinny Howard or the blown up version. But what's weird is his head never seems to lose any of that weight."

Smiling sweetly, Alex jabbed at Howard a little more. "His head can't shrink because it's full of hot air."

Sometimes I wanted to kiss that man of mine right there in public for all the world to see how much I loved him.

"Thanks."

"You know, you haven't told me a thing about our victim's wife yet. I'm depending on you for all the dirt, Poppy," he said with a wink.

Until that moment, I'd completely forgotten the reason we'd come here, other than our coffee addiction. "That's right. Well, the biddies thought Eliza got herself a sugar daddy when she married Samuel because he's quite a bit older than she is. They suspected something nefarious in her wanting him."

Before I could continue, Howard called my name on his way out the door and said, "I want you to get me something on that Morrow story as soon as you can."

Alex cringed and lifted his cup to his mouth to drink the last of his coffee before tossing the cup in the garbage nearby. "Incurable romantics those ladies are. Let's get back to the station and see what Craig's got."

"You don't want to hear any more of the gossip?"

"Save it for later. I'm not in the mood for local nastiness right now."

I finished my coffee and threw away the cup on our way out the door, following Alex across the street to the station. He stopped right before we went into the station and turned to face me with a look so serious on his face.

"You know, Poppy, when we get married, if you don't want to continue working for Howard at *The Eagle*, you can quit at any time. Don't think you need to stay there a minute longer than you want to."

His words stunned me for a moment, and I just stood there in front of the police station like a deer caught in headlights. Quit my job? The thought had never occurred to me. Well, not the idea of quitting because I was married and didn't have to work anymore. I'd considered quitting the newspaper many times over Howard's nastiness and ignorance, but this was different.

Did Alex expect me to not work after we married? Was that what he meant by that?

I opened my mouth to ask him just those questions, but before I could get the words out, he simply walked into the building. Still surprised by his offer, I followed him in and found him just as he got to his office.

He sat down behind his desk and began typing on his laptop like usual, but nothing felt normal as I stood there with those questions filling my head. He didn't act like anything he'd said should make me wonder, but I needed to get to the bottom of this right now.

"Alex, what did you mean—"

Just then, Craig walked in, interrupting me. "Hi guys. The fingerprint guys said their report shouldn't take too long, and Donny called to say he wanted us all to meet early tomorrow morning. I guess he thinks we all work Sundays like he does."

Alex looked up at him and nodded. "Okay. Good work. Is there something else going on tomorrow morning that means you can't be here to meet with him?"

"Katy and I go to church at nine. I just worried that might conflict with Donny's plans," Craig said quietly.

For a moment, Alex sat silently. He would never tell anyone not to attend church services, even though he wasn't a churchgoing man, but a meeting with the coroner might be important enough to miss services one Sunday.

"I'll tell you what. You handle telling Samuel Morrow's widow the news and I'll bring you up to speed on what Donny had to report later tomorrow. Sound good?"

Craig nodded and smiled. "Sure, but I thought you did that already."

"No, she's out of town until around dinnertime, so I'd suggest stopping by around five tonight. We don't want her hearing anything from anyone in town before we speak to her."

"Okay. Sounds good!" Craig said before leaving us alone.

I sat down in front of Alex's desk in my usual seat intent on finding out the answers to my questions but curious as to why he wanted Craig to inform Eliza Morrow of Samuel's death. Never before had Alex pushed that off on a fellow officer.

"Why do you want Craig to tell her instead of us?" I asked as he typed away on his computer.

He stopped and looked over the desk at me. "He needs practice with that facet of the job too. That's all."

"Really? What if she's a suspect?"

"If she's a suspect, we'll find out. Craig needs to be able to learn that part of the job because he won't always be working with me on cases like this."

What did he mean by that? That was the third thing

he'd said that I wasn't sure about, but I chalked that comment up to the reality that Craig and Alex wouldn't always be partnered.

After sitting for a few minutes in silence as Alex caught up on paperwork, I decided it was time to broach the subject that had surprised me just a few minutes ago.

"So can we talk about what you said outside?"

Without missing a beat, he continued to work and asked, "What about it?"

"Well, what you said stopped me in my tracks, to be honest. What did you mean that I can quit my job if I want to? Don't you expect me to work after we get married? Because I'm not sure I'm the stay-at-home type of woman, to be honest, Alex."

His fingers stilled on the keyboard for a moment, and he looked over at me with a confused expression. "What are you talking about? All I said was that if you don't want to work at the newspaper, you don't have to. I didn't say you had to quit. Just that I wouldn't have a problem with it if you did."

"But that's not the way it sounded. It sounded like you were thinking I might be a stay-at-home wife, and now I'm wondering if that means I won't be working with you on cases anymore."

A sweet smile spread across his lips, lighting up his face. Shaking his head, he said, "No, that's not what I meant at all, Poppy. As far as I'm concerned, everything you do now can continue as long as you want it to. I just wanted you to know that if working for that boss of yours gets to a point where it's too much, you don't have to work for him anymore. I'm fine with whatever you want to do. I promise I don't plan to be the type of husband you're thinking of."

"Really? Because I don't want anything to change once we're married. We'll still be the same people we've always been, right?"

Alex nodded. "Right. As far as I'm concerned, the only time I'd want you to stop doing anything with me on cases is once children come. Until then, I don't see why anything should change."

For the second time in less than an hour, Alex's words stunned me. Once children come? We'd never actually discussed having children. I had always just assumed if we were blessed with a child, then we'd have one. But now that he'd mentioned it in the same breath as it being a reason that we wouldn't work together anymore, I wasn't sure I wanted a child as soon as he might.

Children.

Suddenly, everything felt like it was changing.

Chapter Four

A FTER STARING AT the TV for an hour but not really watching anything, I looked over at my phone on the nightstand and saw it was only 10:03. Alex lay sleeping next to me, blissfully unaware of how difficult he'd made my day and now my night with his casual comments that morning. I'd wanted to discuss more about both of them all day, but between work and wedding business that seemed to crop up every day, by the time I got the chance to broach the subject, he'd already fallen fast asleep, leaving me to stew about what he'd said all on my own.

I couldn't just lay there pretending to watch some show I didn't care about, so I slid out from under the covers and headed downstairs to get a drink of water. Maybe that would help me get to sleep.

The stairs creaked as I tiptoed over each one, hoping to not wake Alex. In truth, I wouldn't have been upset if he woke up because then I might get a chance to talk to him about what he'd said. Yes, he'd claimed that he didn't expect me to quit my job and stay home once we were married, but did he mean it? He routinely had a way of saying something and later when he had a chance to give a fuller explanation saying something different.

I poured myself a glass of cold water from the pitcher in the refrigerator and sat down at the kitchen table. Looking up at the clock above the sink, I saw it was now 10:07. Time never flew when you had things on your mind.

As I sat there rehashing everything Alex had said, it dawned on me that my father would still be at the bar and more than happy to talk at this time of night. Saturday nights tended to be busy at McGuire's, but he'd surely pull himself away from his customers for a few minutes to talk to his only daughter.

I tiptoed back up the stairs and dressed as silently as I could in a pair of jeans and a t-shirt before setting off on my short walk to McGuire's Bar. Cars lined the street in front and the tiny parking lot my father had put in at the end of March behind the building in the yard he never used anyway. Clearly, his second annual Cinco de Mayo celebration a week before had continued to bring in residual business.

He stood at the far end of the bar talking to a few of his regulars, so he didn't immediately see me when I walked in. I snuck behind the bar and came up behind him, much to the delight of his customers who kept my appearance a secret so I could surprise him.

Tapping him on the shoulder, I calmly asked, "What's up, Dad?"

His reaction was priceless. He tossed the bar rag in his hands straight up in the air and nearly knocked me over when he spun around, his eyes wide as saucers with a mixture of fear and shock.

"Poppy! You scared me half to death! Don't do that to me."

The men at the bar in front of us laughed so hard

they nearly fell off their barstools, but my surprise had been a cruel joke, so I quickly apologized. "I'm sorry, Dad. I was just trying to have a little fun. I didn't mean to give you a heart attack."

He bent down to pick up the bar rag and began cleaning the space in front of his friends. "You should be more careful. I'm the guy who's walking you down the aisle. You need me to stay alive for a few more weeks."

I wrapped my arms around him and kissed the side of his face. "I need you to stay alive for much longer than that, Dad. But you're tough. No checking out on me yet."

"I have no plans to, honey," he said, tilted his head so it pressed against mine.

"Good."

"So what brings you to the bar tonight? Where's Alex?" my father asked, looking around for my other half.

"He's home sleeping. I didn't want to wake him, and to be honest, I wanted to speak to you in private, if that's okay. Do you have a couple minutes you can spare?"

My father stopped cleaning the bar and looked at me with concern in his eyes. "Sure. Everything okay?"

I waved away his worries and smiled. "Oh yeah. Everything's fine."

"Okay. Let's go into the storeroom. It's quieter in there," he said, guiding me toward the door nearby.

Two cases of vodka provided me with a good place to sit, but my father chose to remain standing, probably still worried that my need to talk that night meant something bad had happened. The man knew me too well.

Folding his arms across his chest, he took a deep

breath and let it out slowly before asking, "So what's this about, Elizabeth?"

Oh, he definitely thought something was wrong if he was using my given name. That was reserved for when I got into trouble or when he was worried, both of which usually happened at the same time.

I smiled and put my hand up to stop him. "It's okay, Dad. It's not an Elizabeth kind of talk. I just wanted to talk to someone tonight about something."

His posture eased just a little. "Well, that tells me a lot. Talk to someone about something. Want to give me some more details? I might be able to help if I knew what you were talking about."

For a moment, I tried to find a way to explain what Alex had said and why it had bothered me so much, but nothing I came up with sounded right. "Well...I guess it's going to sound stupid saying it."

My father stared at me, waiting for some specific details. Finally, when I continued to hedge, he said, "What's going on, honey? I've never seen you at a loss for words like this. Whatever the problem is, just talk about it and I'm sure you'll see it's not that bad."

I was sure he was right. If I just unburdened myself, it would be much better.

"Alex and I were talking today. You know, just talking like we usually do."

When I stopped, my father nodded and tried to encourage me to continue. "Well, that's what people do, especially people who are planning to marry in a few weeks. Is this about the wedding, Poppy?"

Now even I began to feel frustrated at my inability to get the words out. Standing, I began to pace back and forth between the cases of liquor and kegs of beer. "No, it's not about the wedding. Everything's fine with that. Well, except for the fact that we still haven't decided on what we're going to be serving and we have to pick the cake out on Monday. But it's not about the wedding. No, that's fine."

"That's good, honey. I'm glad to hear it. Then what's wrong?" my father asked, worry lacing each word.

I walked to the back of the storeroom and turned around to face him, stopping next to a case of champagne he kept for special occasions. "Alex said that if I don't want to work at the newspaper after we get married that I don't have to. That I can quit."

The serious way I said those words made it sound like some grand pronouncement. I waited for my father to react, but for a moment, he said nothing, as if he was expecting me to continue with something more.

Finally, he said, "Well, that's nice. Howard has become more difficult with you in the past few months, putting more and more demands on you to report things about cases he knows he shouldn't ask about, so I can see where Alex would think that could be something you'd like."

"I guess. But then he said something about me not working with him on cases anymore. I hated even hearing him say that."

A look of surprise settled into my father's features. "Are you sure that's what he meant, Poppy? That he doesn't want you working with him on cases once you're married?"

Shifting my weight from one foot to the other, I admitted that wasn't exactly what he'd said. "Well, he probably didn't mean it that way. He mentioned that once we have children that he wouldn't want me to still work on cases with him too."

I looked down at the floor as I waited to hear my father's response to that, but once again he didn't immediately say anything. Lifting my head, I saw him smiling, as if anything I'd said was good.

"What?" I asked, disappointed the person I'd chosen to bear my soul to didn't see how important this was to me.

"Poppy, I'm not sure what's troubling you. I can completely understand Alex not wanting his wife and the mother of his child or children working on murder cases. Having children changes things. I'm sure you know that."

"I know, but I don't want things to change yet. I love working with him on cases. I've never enjoyed anything as much in my life as what we do to solve crimes. Why does that have to go away?"

My father waved me over toward him, so I walked back to my seat on the vodka cases and sat down. He smiled at me, like he would when I was a little girl and he wanted to tell me something he knew I had to hear.

"Honey, what's this about? Are you saying you don't want to have children with Alex? If so, that's something he deserves to know before marrying you."

His question shocked me. Once the surprise of his words wore off and I could speak again, I asked, "What? Why would you say that?"

"It sounds like that's what you're saying. You want to continue solving cases with him. You can't do that and have children at the same time."

"Of course I want to have kids with Alex. Why wouldn't I? I love him, Dad."

"Then what's this all about, Poppy, if it isn't about children?" he asked pointedly, not letting me squirm out of telling him the truth.

The problem was I didn't know why giving up solving cases with Alex in exchange for having a child didn't thrill me. I loved the idea of a baby in my life, a little boy with deep brown eyes like his father's and his serious nature or a little girl with my spunk and silliness.

So why did the mere mention of our work arrangement ending once a child came along make me sad?

"I don't know what this is about. I don't. I just know as soon as he mentioned me not coming out with him on cases anymore, I felt lost. I love Alex and I do want children, but does everything have to change so quickly? Can't we at least have a little time with it just the two of us after we get back from the honeymoon?"

My father nodded his understanding and smiled once again. "Of course. Maybe you should talk to Alex about this. I get the sense you haven't yet."

"No, I haven't. I wanted to, but things kept coming up all day, and then he fell asleep early, so I didn't get a chance to."

"I have a feeling once you mention it to him you'll see he probably wants that honeymoon period too. You're both young. You have a lot of time to think about kids. In the meantime, just be happy that you found each other. I've been thinking about that these past few months. Your mother would be so happy to see you found someone who deserves everything you can give."

Standing, I wrapped my arms around his shoulders and hugged him to me. "I wish she could have met him. She would like him."

"She'd love him because she'd see he loves you. It's obvious from the first moment you see him looking at you. The sun rises and sets on you for him."

I leaned back and saw sadness in my father's eyes. "Don't worry, Dad. I'll still be your little girl, even after I'm married."

He cupped my face in his calloused hands and nodded. "As your mother used to say, a son is a son until he takes a wife. But a daughter is a daughter all her life. You'll always be my little girl, Poppy."

Tears began to well in my eyes, so I quickly joked to lighten the mood. "I better get going. Alex probably woke up and is wandering around the house confused where I am. You still need me to work next Thursday?"

My father's hands slid from my face as he shook his head. "No. Katy said she could work after all, but you know you're always welcome behind the bar whenever you want to come by. This place is as much yours as it is mine, to be honest. It's McGuire's, after all."

"Okay, well I might come over anyway and bug you and Katy for a few hours that night. I've been missing hanging out and seeing the regulars. I'll call you tomorrow after the cake tasting and let you know how it went, okay?"

He kissed me on the forehead and chuckled. "Cake tasting. As if anyone cares how wedding cake tastes anyway. People are either too drunk once the cake is cut and handed out or gone home."

I rolled my eyes at his old fashioned ways. "I love you, Dad. Talk to you later."

As I began to walk toward the door out of the storeroom, he said, "Hey, be careful. I know it's only a few blocks, but you guys haven't found Samuel

Morrow's killer yet. You still have that pepper spray Alex gave you?"

The pepper spray sat at the bottom of my purse back on my bedroom dresser, but my father didn't need to know that. Lying, I nodded and avoided his gaze as I said, "Yeah, yeah. This is still Sunset Ridge, Dad. I'll be fine. Talk to you later."

AS MUCH AS my father liked to think our hometown had become some dangerous place, I didn't worry about walking home in the dark. My gut told me whoever killed poor Samuel Morrow wasn't some mass murderer beginning a crime spree. Just as with every other murder Alex and I had investigated, the likely killer was someone close to him who had motives unknown to us.

When I crossed Barn Street to get to the side my house was on, I did think about the fact that my wedding band was the only piece of jewelry taken from Samuel's entire store. Thank God my father didn't know that detail or he would have insisted I have an escort the few blocks home.

It had rained while I was at McGuire's, so the light from the streetlights reflected off the puddles along the sidewalk as I headed home. The air smelled fresh and clean, like it always did after it rained. I took a deep breath in and held it inside my lungs for a moment before letting it out in a rush.

I saw the bedroom light on through the window and began to hurry toward the house, hoping Alex hadn't awoken while I was gone and now worried I'd suddenly disappeared from the bed we shared. Breaking into a jog, I reached the house and took the front steps by two, but as I stepped onto the porch out of the corner of my eye I saw something move in the bushes on the side of my house.

Too big to be a cat or dog, it looked like a figure crouching in the shadows. I called out, "Hello? Who's there?" but no one answered.

Suddenly frightened, I hurried to unlock the front door and rushed inside, slamming the door behind me. As I stood there, my heart beating like a jackhammer in my chest, I saw something move outside through the living room window.

Was this just my mind playing tricks on me?

"Alex, are you up? Can you come down here right now, please?" I yelled upstairs, still frozen on the spot where I'd seen the figure from inside the house.

In seconds, he raced down the stairs and appeared before me in just his pants and shoes, his eyes filled with fear from my panicked plea. "What is it, Poppy? What happened?"

"I was walking home from my father's bar and just as I got in front of the house, I saw something or someone in the bushes. I hurried inside and I saw the figure run along the side of the house as I stood right here."

Pointing out the living room window, I said, "It ran right under the window."

Immediately, he sprang into action. "Wait here while I go outside to check it out. I need a flashlight."

He rushed into the kitchen to get one and then returned to go out the front door. I followed him outside, and just a few steps onto the porch he turned around to look at me angrily.

"I just told you to stay inside."

"I'm not sure I'm crazy about this Cro-Magnon attitude you've taken on. I'm coming with you."

Alex sighed and shook his head. "I don't think it's Cro-Magnon to want to protect the woman you love, Poppy."

I took his hand and brought it to my lips to kiss it. "And I love you for it. But let's go see what we can find."

We walked around the side of the house next to the driveway, and Alex pointed the flashlight back and forth along the ground as we searched for any clue as to who or what could have been hiding in the shadows.

In the soil near the bushes under the living room window, Alex noticed a fresh footprint. He crouched down and shined the light on it. "This looks pretty fresh."

He looked back at my feet and then at the footprint. "I'm going to assume your feet didn't make this."

His lame attempt at a joke amused me. "Not my size sevens. Those are bigger than my feet by a few inches."

"Mine too."

He took his phone out and snapped a picture of the footprint before standing up and heading toward the backyard. I followed closely behind him and we searched the property, but we didn't find anything more than that single footprint.

Alex shrugged and flashed the light around the yard one last time. "Whatever it was, they probably ran through the grass, which is why there don't seem to be any other footprints."

"Do you think it was a they and not an it?" I asked, suddenly wanting to be back inside and cozy under the covers in bed.

"I don't know. Let's go back in," he said calmly as he

turned toward the house.

"Are you going to call in the forensic guys from the state police?" I asked as we walked back inside.

My question made him smile, and he shook his head. "They have no reason to come out. There's been no crime."

"But can't you pull some strings? You know, throw your weight around and call in some favors."

He stopped and looked at me, shining the light in my direction. "For what? Someone walking through the yard?"

I had to admit that there had been no crime to investigate, but the whole episode had put me on edge. We went back into the house and upstairs to the bedroom to get back to watching our movie, but I didn't feel as safe as I had when I'd left just an hour before.

Snuggling up next to Alex, I admitted how frightened it all had made me. "I know I shouldn't worry, but after Samuel Morrow's murder and my ring being the only piece of jewelry taken from his store, I'm freaked out."

He pressed a kiss to the top of my head and whispered, "I'm sure the two events are unrelated. Don't worry. I'm not going to let anything happen to my bride right before her wedding day. If someone wants to get to you, they're going to have to go through me."

I sighed and closed my eyes as I lay my head on his chest. He wrapped his arm around me and gave me a gentle squeeze to reassure me I had nothing to fear. I'd never felt as safe and secure in my life as I did in Alex's arms. As I slowly drifted off to sleep, I wished no one would want to get either of us.

Chapter Five

BRIGHT AND EARLY the next morning, Alex and I arrived at the police station ready to tackle the Samuel Morrow case. We had no suspects as of yet—well, none that Alex had mentioned to me—but what we did have was the intense desire to bring Samuel's killer to justice.

So with coffees in hand and dogged determination, we gathered in his office with Craig to begin the investigation in earnest.

Alex opened his notebook and looked across his desk at Craig, who sat to my left. "So, how did the widow take the news last night?"

Craig made an uncomfortable noise that sounded like someone elbowed him in the gut. "It wasn't my favorite part of the day. I'll tell you that."

I patted him on the forearm in a gesture of sympathy. "It gets easier. I promise."

My reassuring words seemed to help a little, and he nodded. "I hope so. I mean, I guess it could have been worse. She didn't break down or fall apart, so at least there was that."

"So what happened?" Alex asked, uncharacteristically impatient with his junior partner.

"She came to the door, and the maid told her the police had been there earlier in the day. I tried to be as gentle as possible, considering I had to tell her that her husband had been murdered that morning. She listened to everything I had to say and then cried a little. Then she said she needed to call someone, so I left."

"Okay. Sounds pretty typical," Alex said, jotting down a note in his tablet. "Anything else you think we should all know about that whole interaction?"

Craig looked over at me with terror in his eyes and then back at Alex. "Like what?"

Lifting his head, Alex smiled. "Like what did you feel in your gut about the entire thing? Did she look genuinely unhappy to hear her husband had been murdered? Did you get the feeling she knew before you told her? I mean, the man was dead for nearly half a day before we got to meet with her and break the news. So what did your gut tell you?"

I watched as Craig swallowed hard and thought that what his gut was telling him at that moment was that it presently planned to send his breakfast back up. He looked like everything Alex had asked terrified him.

"Uh, I don't know. I wasn't exactly thinking about that kind of stuff when I was telling her," he answered quietly. "I'm sorry."

Hoping to rescue him and save us all from him getting sick all over the place, I squeezed his arm to calm him. "It's okay. Just think back to what you thought at that moment, even if it wasn't a conscious idea going through your head. For example, did her crying seem more like crocodile tears than real crying? Were there actual tears?"

Craig remained silent for a long moment before

shaking his head. "I think they were real, but I do have to say I expected more. I know if someone told me that Katy was murdered, I'd be inconsolable."

"Okay, that's good. A cop's instincts are invaluable," Alex said, easing Craig's worry. "So do you think she knew before you told her?"

"Hmmm...I'm not sure. I didn't get a sense of complete shock from her when I broke the news."

"Interesting. Good work, Craig. Do we know anything else about her and our victim? Were they happy? Any problems? He was a bit older than her, so anything going on?"

Craig shook his head, so Alex looked at me. "Anything the local gossips can contribute to this?"

"So you've had a change of heart?" I teased.

"You know the gossips in this town. Not that I put a lot of stock into what they think of people, but as they say, a clock is right at least twice a day. I did warn you I'd be asking about it before."

I hated to confess that I had heard something about Samuel and Eliza Morrow in front of Craig. Sheepishly, I admitted, "Well, I don't put my faith in what the gossips say, but I have heard rumors of issues, let's say."

"Rumors?" Alex asked, cocking an eyebrow in interest.

Both Alex and Craig stared at me as I figured out how to explain what I'd heard. The gossips always whispered about the Morrows because she was so much younger than he was and very much a flirty woman compared to her husband, who was always far more serious whenever he was seen in public.

Not that I ever thought any of it meant they were having troubles in their marriage. But the gossips did.

"Well, I've heard murmurings about her especially. That he was her sugar daddy, like I told you about yesterday. I have no evidence to support that, though. To me it was always a wild rumor. I've never met her officially. I've only seen her in passing. I don't even think I've ever seen Samuel and his wife together."

Alex twisted his face into a grimace, even though he'd asked for the local gossip. "Could be sour grapes. These local gossips aren't exactly young women in the prime of their lives. Maybe they're jealous. I don't think I've ever seen Mrs. Morrow that I know of. Is she drop dead gorgeous?"

I tilted my head back and forth trying to decide how to describe Eliza Morrow. Tall and willowy, like many wealthy women I'd met, she had shoulder length black hair that would have looked too severe on other women but looked gorgeous next to her deep olive skin. The combination gave her a rather exotic look, and her dark brown eyes completed the effect.

But something about her always seemed off when I caught a glimpse of her on the street. I didn't know if it was her nose, which seemed slightly too big for her face, or the sharply angular structure of her jaw. Whatever it was, I didn't know if I'd call her gorgeous or even beautiful.

"Not drop dead gorgeous, but definitely striking," I said, comfortable with how I'd categorized her without sounding catty.

Alex switched his focus to Craig and asked him, "What do you think?"

"She's not my type, but I'd go with striking. She's a little...um..." he hesitated for a moment before completing his thought. "A little severe looking for me, I think."

"I'm intrigued," Alex said with a chuckle. "I'm having a hard time picturing Samuel Morrow with a woman anyone would describe as striking and severe. He had a very average look going, so this is interesting. Maybe it was a sugar daddy thing for her."

"What do we know about their background?" I asked Craig.

Opening up his notebook to the page with notes on the case, he began explaining what he'd found. "Eliza Morrow is forty-seven, and she's fifteen years younger than her husband. Neither one of them were born in Sunset Ridge. He was a New Yorker and she was born in the Washington D.C. area. They married before they came to town in 1992. Samuel Morrow made a lot of money in diamonds in the eighties. He considered moving to Sunset Ridge as retiring. As far as I can tell, his wife has never held a job since they moved here. She doesn't do much with local events, but she and her husband are always mentioned as donors to anything done through fundraising in town."

Craig's report that Eliza was only forty-seven surprised me. I would have put her at a few years older, to be honest.

"Well, her disinterest in attending all those local events is probably another reason the gossips who speak with forked tongues don't like her," Alex said with a huff of disgust. "Okay, so what do we all think about her as a suspect?"

His question surprised both Craig and me, and we looked at each other, our shocked expressions matching one another. It wasn't like Alex to jump to conclusions like that. Nothing we'd learned so far had indicated Eliza

Morrow should be considered a suspect in her husband's death.

So I asked the obvious question.

"What makes you think she's a suspect, Alex?"

He shrugged nonchalantly. "It's customary to look at the spouse first in cases like this. That's all."

That may have been all, but there still seemed to be something strange beneath his words.

"So Eliza Morrow is our first suspect?" Craig asked in a confused voice.

Alex nodded. "For now. Let's say she's someone to keep in mind. What else do we know about Samuel?"

Craig opened his mouth to say something, but nothing came out. Finally, he said, "I don't have much. He owned that jewelry store of his since 1992. Although other stores have gone out of business in the last decade or so, his is one of the few that have remained and continues to do well. As far as the man himself, I've never heard anyone say a bad word about him around town."

I chimed in to add, "Me neither. Everyone loved Samuel Morrow. He wasn't just a jeweler, though. He was a jewelry designer, and a good one. Just the other day Mrs. Jacobs showed me her pendant he created for her using the diamond from her engagement ring to her second husband. It's beautiful."

"Mrs. Jacobs? The lady who has had two husbands in the past three years?" Craig asked with a chuckle. "I'm going on the record right here and now that we're going to have a case involving her at some point in the future. I don't know if it will be her or one of her husbands, but I'm betting on her."

I nudged his arm and laughed. "I think the saying is

hell hath no fury like a woman scorned. It says nothing about men."

"Trust me. Men don't need a saying. I've been doing this job long enough to know anyone scorned is a dangerous person," Alex said in a serious voice, bringing down the mood of the room.

The three of us sat there in silence as the horrible truth of what he said hung in the air. Love made people do crazy things, and losing love made them do even crazier things.

Quietly, Craig asked, "Do you think the whole scorned woman thing is important to this case?"

I had a feeling he had gotten lost in our riffing back and forth, so I shook my head and smiled. "No way. Why would Eliza Morrow be scorned? Samuel was a loyal husband."

Completely sidestepping our detour into our killer being a scorned woman out to get Samuel for some slight in romance, Alex asked Craig, "What did the fingerprint guys find at the scene?"

"Not a thing. Nothing but our victim's fingerprints on a few jewelry boxes in the back. Not a single print on any of the glass cases, the register, or any of the other nearly five hundred boxes of things he had in the storeroom. It's as if only Samuel had ever been in that store."

Pursing his lips, Alex nodded. "Hmmm. Our killer wiped the place down before he or she left. What about the other store owners on that street? Did they see anything or anyone suspicious around the time Samuel was killed? A gunshot isn't something that goes unnoticed."

"Unless a silencer was used," I added, garnering a

frown in return for my contribution to the conversation.

"I spoke to all the store owners on that part of Main Street, and none of them heard anything," Craig said. "They were surprised down to the last man that anything like this had happened basically right under their noses. Maybe Poppy's right and a silencer was used."

"We'll get to that if and when we find out that no one really heard a thing. For now, I'm keeping my skeptical mind open. What else do we know?"

Craig and I sat there silently looking at Alex and likely thinking the same thing but not wanting to say anything about it. At least I knew I was thinking about it.

My ring.

But maybe it wasn't that simple. Maybe there was another explanation for what happened to my ring.

I cleared my voice and said, "I know no one wants to talk about what happened with my ring, but I was thinking that maybe it wasn't as simple as the killer had stolen it or had even killed Samuel to get it. Maybe he had to send it somewhere to get the design just right. Or maybe it's in one of those hundreds of boxes. It doesn't necessarily have to be in the same box as your ring or even anywhere close to it."

Neither man uttered a word after I finished, and the longer the silence continued, the more I felt like I was the only one who believed the theft of my ring and Samuel's death could be unconnected. I knew it didn't sound plausible to them, but I needed to believe there was some other reason than my wedding band for Samuel's murder.

Finally, Alex gave me what I knew was a forced smile and said, "That's a good point, Poppy. Craig, I'm going to need you to check all those boxes and all of Samuel's files to see if he had sent any pieces of jewelry out to another store in the past two weeks. Let's see what we can find out about where that ring could be."

"Okay. I'll get on that right now," Craig said, quickly standing up as if he now couldn't wait to leave.

Alex's office phone rang, so he held up his hand to stop Craig for the moment and answered it. "Hello?"

Pressing his lips together, he hummed for a second or two as he listened to the caller before saying, "Let me put you on speaker, Donny. I think Craig and Poppy should hear this."

We leaned forward toward the black phone on the desk in front of us and waited for the coroner to repeat what had made Alex sound so serious just moments before. Had he found something other than the gunshot wound that we needed to know about?

Donny's voice intoned through the speaker, booming out at us. "So the gang's all there, huh? Good. Let's me kill a bunch of birds with one stone."

At times, his sense of humor just felt wrong. While the vision of all those dead birds lying on the ground around him in a pool of their own blood marched through my mind, I decided now was one of those times.

"Well, I have news for you all. That gunshot wound to Samuel Morrow's head wasn't the cause of death."

Donny paused for effect and to let his stunning announcement sink in and then continued. "Now that I have your attention, I can tell you that I have the actual cause of death. Samuel Morrow died from a fractured larynx."

All three of us looked at the phone wide-eyed as his last words resonated in our heads. He died from what?

"Can you say that again, Donny?" Alex asked, his voice full of shock at this news.

The coroner chuckled, as if any of this was funny in the least. "I said he died from a fractured larynx. The gunshot to the center of his forehead didn't kill him. My guess is that your killer thought they'd throw us off the real reason he died."

"Someone can actually die from an injury to the larynx? Was Samuel strangled then?" I asked, vaguely recollecting something I saw on a TV show once.

"Nope. Not strangled. His hyoid bone wasn't broken."

"Then how did he die, Donny?" Alex asked, his voice full of frustration from the coroner's need to present his findings like this was some reality murder mystery show.

"So impatient. Okay, here goes. My best guess after my initial examination is that a single swift blow to your victim's neck fractured his larynx. Usually, I'd say this is pretty rare because the whole larynx is one big area of cartilage, joints, and muscle, so it's pretty flexible. But as we get older, like the rest of the body, that area gets less flexible. A sharp, hard hit to the front of the neck and bam! It's game over then, unless you get medical help immediately."

I looked across the desk at Alex, who looked like he had no idea what to make of this. Rarely had I seen him look so perplexed.

"I've seen people get hit in the neck dozens of times, Donny. Why did this kill Samuel? Isn't the larynx just the voice box?"

"It is, but your larynx can fracture, and once that happens, it's only a matter of time before you die because you can't get air in. It's really that simple. The human body is an amazing machine that can handle a lot of stress, but in this case, that one stressor on the larynx was too much and he died from it."

"So he died from lack of oxygen?"

"Yes. And he wouldn't have been able to cry out because his voice box wouldn't have been working. Why someone then felt the need to shoot him in the head seems strange, but I'll leave that up to you to figure out why," Donny said.

Almost as an afterthought, he added, "Oh, and the gun used was a .45, although it seems like overkill to shoot a man you just killed. I'll let you know if I find anything else interesting."

Donny hung up, and Alex pressed the speaker button to end the call before looking across the desk at Craig and me. It felt like everything we'd been thinking about this case had just been upended.

Who would have wanted to kill Samuel so violently, and then shoot him afterward?

"Well, that was interesting, to say the least. Any ideas?"

The two of us sat there and shook our heads. I had no idea where to begin with this case. Then, one idea popped into my head.

"I think we might be able to safely rule out Eliza Morrow. From what Donny said, the blow to Samuel's neck had to be pretty strong. I don't think she has the kind of strength necessary for that."

Out of the corner of my eye, I saw Craig nod, but Alex didn't seem so convinced. Shaking his head, he frowned. "I'm not ruling anyone out as of now. I've been doing this for years, and this is the first time I've run into death by broken larynx. If that can happen, then I'm thinking anything can happen, including a forty-seven year old woman killing her sixty-two year old husband with one swift blow to his neck."

I didn't know why Alex suddenly seemed so intent on believing that a woman who had been married to a man for twenty-five years would kill her husband in such a way. In fact, he seemed strangely fascinated by the idea that their marriage wasn't what it seemed to be on the outside, even though nothing either of them ever showed the world indicated any trouble whatsoever.

"Okay, well, I'm going to get on those boxes and files and leave you guys to it," Craig said before hurrying out and leaving us alone.

"So what's our first move?" I asked, silently suspecting I already knew the first person he wanted to speak to.

"Let's go see this striking widow and see what we can find out from her. I also want to talk to the local gossips on this one."

Surprised to hear he once again had a use for them, I asked, "Why?"

He winked at me and stood from behind his desk. "In matters of love in this town, I've seen that those ladies seem to have a pretty good track record. In fact, the only person they've ever been wrong about is you, Poppy. I can't hold that against them forever, especially when what they have to say might help us solve a case, can I?"

As I followed him out of his office, I thought to myself that he was right. That didn't mean I took what they had to say with anything more than a grain of salt, though.

Chapter Six

WE PULLED UP to the grey and blue Victorian known around town as the Morrow Home, and Alex turned off the car but didn't make a move to get out. I sat there in the passenger seat silently wondering what was holding him up since he seemed to be just staring blankly out the front window. When he didn't move for a full minute, I figured it was time to say something.

"What's up? You look a million miles away," I said, pushing on his bicep to give him a nudge.

"Hang on," he said curtly, practically brushing me off.

I grudgingly did as he ordered and looked around to see what he could be looking at. He'd seen this neighborhood countless times, so that couldn't be it, unless he'd had a complete change of heart about the section of town he called Victorian Row and was checking out one of the homes as a potential buyer. I dismissed that idea as quickly as it came into my head, sure that Alex didn't plan to have us become residents of this section of Sunset Ridge.

Other than homes and their perfectly manicured lawns and landscaping that cost a small fortune, I didn't see anything else that would have attracted his attention. There wasn't a soul out walking their dog or tending to their award winning flower gardens on this beautiful May day.

Then I remembered what day it was. Sunday. Checking my phone, I saw it wasn't yet eleven. That explained why the streets were empty. Everyone still sat in church.

"If you're wondering where everyone is, I can tell you it's nothing worth your time. There's no mystery here."

Alex nodded but didn't turn his head to even look at me as he said, "Church. Yeah."

"Okay," I mumbled, feeling a bit put off by his behavior.

Then, as if someone had lifted a veil from over him, he smiled and looked over at me. "Ready to go in?"

He moved to get out of the car, but I grabbed a hold of his right arm to stop him. "No way. You don't get to act all weird like that for the last five minutes and then pretend like none of it ever happened. What was going on with you? Why were you just staring off into space like that?"

"What do you mean? I was just getting a feel for the place," he said in his most casual tone.

I closed my fist around his sleeve to keep him from bolting since that answer told me nothing. "That's nonsense, and you know it. You've been to this part of town enough that you don't need to get a feel for anything. So what were you doing?"

A slow smile spread across his lips. "Okay, fine. I was watching a man in the driveway at the Morrow's house."

Turning my head, I looked out the window toward

the side of the house and saw the man Alex had been watching there washing a silver Mercedes. He had to be at least six feet tall and had arms that looked like they could crush coconuts they were so muscular. The man had a military look to him because of his closely cropped light brown hair and the serious look he wore.

"Who is he?" I asked, even though I doubted Alex knew the answer any more than I did.

"From what I've seen him do so far, my only guesses are car wash boy or driver."

I replayed what the maid had told us yesterday when we came to break the news to Eliza Morrow. She hadn't mentioned anyone driving her employer, just that she had gone to D.C. for the day.

"Do you think he works for the Morrows?" I asked, suddenly quite protective of Samuel's home in his absence because of the strange, very muscular man who stood outside it hosing down the car like some guy posing for one of those beefcake calendars.

"I have no idea, but he caught my attention. I wonder if he's caught anyone else's," Alex said with a knowing grin.

Of course he'd caught others' attention. This was Sunset Ridge, after all.

"Let's go in and speak to Mrs. Morrow."

As we walked up the sidewalk to the front door, I snuck one more look at the man still rinsing off the car near the garage. I guessed he couldn't be more than twenty-five. Maybe twenty-six, at most.

"Should I be worried that my fiancé can't take her eyes off some guy?" Alex asked.

I snapped my head in his direction and saw him smiling. "No. Don't be silly. I actually just feel really bothered by the fact that there's a man in Samuel Morrow's driveway. Even if it's completely innocent, it looks bad. I don't like that."

"Maybe it's like you said, completely innocent. I never got the feeling Samuel cared what others thought of him anyway."

The two of us stepped up onto the porch and I said, "Well, it still bugs me. I don't like the idea of people thinking this guy has replaced Samuel already. It's just not right."

Alex nodded and rang the doorbell. I wanted to be understanding because I understood what it felt like to lose someone close to you, but part of me wanted to tell Eliza Morrow that her decision to let whoever that guy was stand outside and wash the car looked bad.

"I get that you're upset by him, so let me do the talking in here, okay?" Alex said just as the front door opened.

"Fine. I'm not really feeling like I'm in a talking mood much right now anyway," I grumbled, leaning back to try to see what that guy was doing now.

The woman we spoke to yesterday appeared in the doorway. "Yes? Can I help you?"

"We'd like to speak to Mrs. Morrow," Alex said sweetly. "Can you please tell her Officer Alex Montero and his partner Poppy McGuire are here?"

The maid hesitated for a moment before remembering her job was to do exactly as Alex had asked. Opening the door, she stood back as we walked into the gorgeously designed home. A high-ceilinged foyer spacious enough to fit my first apartment from college flowed into a pale blue room to the left, and as we moved into that space, I had to admit of all the

Victorians I'd been in around town, the Morrows' home surpassed them all.

"I'll let her know you're here," the maid said before leaving us alone in what I was calling in my mind the living room.

I slowly turned around to allow myself to take in all the room's design as Alex sat down on a white high-backed couch trimmed in dark wood. Large bookcases painted in the same pale blue as the rest of the room towered up to the ten foot ceilings and flanked a large portrait of some woman with deep red flowing hair sitting on the edge of a brook. On the opposite wall, a fireplace with a grand wood mantle surround painted white was the focal point around which two burgundy upholstered Queen Anne chairs were arranged along with a dark wood coffee table.

The room showed a deliberate mixture of old and new to accentuate the Victorian architecture of the home while melding more modern furnishings. The result was breathtaking while at the same time cozy. I had to give Eliza credit. She knew how to create a look.

"You look like you're in love, Poppy," Alex said with a chuckle as I continued to take in the room's design. "Should I assume you're going to want to move to one of these Victorians at some point?"

I rolled my eyes and sat down beside him on the couch. "Don't be ridiculous. This is too much for someone like me. I can't even figure out how anyone gets up high enough to dust those top shelves on the bookcase, for God's sake. That said, I can appreciate a beautiful home, and this is stunning."

"I'm glad to hear that. I'm not a big fan of these drafty old places. I like my home to be a bit more intimate."

"I get that, but I can see why someone would want this too. It's gorgeous. She's done an incredible job with this room."

"Thank you, Miss McGuire," a soft voice said, and I turned around to see Eliza Morrow walking behind us toward one of the black modern chairs situated across from us.

Even more willowy in person, Mrs. Morrow seemed to glide over to her seat, her long navy blue top swaying above her beige pants as she moved, giving her an ethereal look. Wearing her black hair pulled back in a classic chignon, she looked more severe than ever before when I saw her, but something in her dark eyes hinted at her being softer than her look made her seem.

Up close to her for the first time, I quickly realized my judgment that her nose was too big had been correct. Not by much, but enough to make her face look imbalanced. It didn't mean she was unattractive, by any means, but it did cause her to look off somehow.

"Officer Montero, my maid told me you came by to see me yesterday to break the news of my husband's death but I wasn't home. I wanted to thank you for that."

Alex nodded and said, "Please let me express my condolences for your loss, Mrs. Morrow. Poppy and I knew Samuel and thought the world of him. Just recently, we'd been working with him designing our wedding bands."

Eliza Morrow smiled warmly in what seemed to be genuine happiness at hearing Alex talk about her late husband. "He had an eye for what was beautiful, to be sure. You gave me the credit for this room, Miss

McGuire, but it was all Samuel. This entire house was his favorite design project," she said, extending a single arm and moving it through the air like a model on a game show displaying that day's prizes.

"It's stunning. His choices for this room are perfect. It's grand and elegant while being welcoming at the same time," I said.

"Your maid told us you were in D.C. when we came yesterday. Did you drive the silver car I saw outside?" Alex asked.

The question seemed to be a strange one, but we did need to know who that man outside was.

Eliza shook her head and frowned. "No. I don't drive. I don't even have a license. I never have. My driver Bruno took me."

So that's who he was. I found it odd at first to hear someone in the twenty-first century didn't drive, but then I thought about how much driving I actually did living in Sunset Ridge. As a small town, it offered almost everything I needed within walking distance. Only the Food King was too far to really walk to.

Perhaps her having a driver to take her places wasn't strange.

"Is that the man I saw outside as I walked up to the house?" Alex asked, once again in a very measured tone.

Her gaze moved to the hallway behind us and then back to Alex. "Yes. His name is Bruno Carter. He's been my driver for two years now. He's a godsend since I don't drive and I never wanted to bother Samuel with driving me whenever I wanted to go anywhere."

"What time did you leave yesterday morning?" Alex asked as he jotted down the word GODSEND next to Bruno's name in his notebook.

When she didn't immediately answer, he stopped writing and looked up at her. "Is something wrong, Mrs. Morrow?"

She drew her dark eyebrows in toward her nose, making her look almost sinister as she glared at him. "I have a feeling you think I had something to do with my husband's death, Officer Montero. Well, I can tell you that I had nothing to do with it. Samuel was a very nice man to me, and I cared for him very much. I would never do anything to hurt him."

Shaking his head, Alex relayed his experience with the spouse being the first person questioned in any case like this. "Mrs. Morrow, I understand what you're going through at this time. I lost my wife years ago, and I was the first one the police came to. It's not that the spouse is necessarily the first suspect, but no one knew your husband better than you, so it's only logical that we start the investigation with you. I hope you can see we mean no disrespect."

I'd seen Alex cajole witnesses, and I'd seen him charm them into telling him exactly what he needed to know. But never was he a better cop than when he showed someone suffering from the loss of a loved one that he truly understood them. Each time he let that part of him be seen, I couldn't help but love him even more.

"Thank you, Officer Montero. I appreciate that," Eliza said quietly, giving him the cue that he could continue with his questions. "Bruno drove me to Georgetown University yesterday. We arrived at ten, and he picked me back up at around three-thirty."

Her answer surprised me. Why would she go to Georgetown on a Saturday in May?

Alex smiled. "Thank you. Why did you go there,

Mrs. Morrow?"

"Why does it matter why I went there? I can have any number of people prove that I was there," she said angrily.

"It's just something we cops have to ask. That way we can rule you out completely. So what were you doing there yesterday for nearly six hours?"

"I was at the library."

Her answer sounded forced and odd, but instead of focusing any more on her, he moved to who else may have wanted to hurt Samuel.

"Do you have any idea who could have wanted to do this to your husband, Mrs. Morrow?" he asked.

She immediately shook her head. "No. Everyone liked Samuel. He was a nice person. He kept to himself, ran his business, and in his spare time, continued to design the interior of this house. There was nothing to dislike about him. I'm sure if you spoke to most people in town you'd find they thought he was a nice person too."

"Have there been any problems with anyone that you can think of? Anyone ever have an issue with him at the store? Even something small could be important. You'd be surprised at what is usually at the bottom of most crimes like this. Something seemingly insignificant to us might have meant the world to someone else."

Eliza Morrow thought for a moment and then shook her head again. "I can't think of anything. He didn't tell me much about the business, so I can't be sure about that, but he didn't mention any problems with anyone recently. In fact, in all the time I knew my husband, I don't think he ever had an issue with another soul."

I listened intently to everything she said, curious as to why she only seemed to describe her late husband of twenty-five years as nice. Of all the adjectives used to show how you felt about a person, none were more tepid than nice. A gift you didn't really want you'd call nice to spare someone's feelings. Food you disliked but didn't want to be rude about was nice.

What did it say about their marriage that the best she could muster up for the man she claimed to care for was to call him nice?

"What about life insurance? Can you tell me what kind of policies Samuel had?" Alex asked with a hint of frustration in his voice.

Eliza Morrow likely didn't pick up on it, but I heard it loud and clear.

"I don't know, but let me check his study. I know he kept important papers in there," she said before walking out of the room.

Alex turned around and watched her leave. When she was gone, he whispered, "What's your initial feeling so far?"

I saw in his dark eyes that he had something in mind already. "I'm not sure. I think I feel bad for Samuel that all his wife can say about him is he was a nice man. I've known you for just over a tenth of the time she knew him and nice is the last thing I'd use to describe you."

He laughed, mistaking my intent with my comment. "Nice. What would you say?"

Tapping him on the arm, I shook my head. "You know what I meant. They were married for a quarter century and all she has to say is he was nice."

He nodded and shrugged his shoulders. "I guess. Maybe we're being too hard on her. Everyone mourns differently. You did say she was severe, and you were right. Maybe she's just a closed off person. It just seems so odd compared to Samuel, who was so gregarious and open."

The whole time he talked, he kept looking out into the hallway at something, but I didn't know why. Finally, I asked, "What's so exciting out there? I'm sure she'll be back any moment."

"It's not her I'm interested in. That driver guy was standing out in the hallway listening the whole time we were talking, but now that's she's gone to Samuel's study, he's disappeared. I want to talk to him before we leave."

"Are you thinking there's something between them?" I asked, surprised since I would have guessed Bruno wouldn't be Eliza's type.

She didn't seem like the kind of woman who would be with a manual laborer kind of guy. And she had to be at least twenty years older than him. Not that Eliza wasn't appealing, in a strident kind of way, but I didn't fully peg them for a couple or her as a cheating wife.

At least I didn't want to.

She returned moments later and sat down with a small stack of papers in her hands. "My husband had a policy at Maryland Life for one million on himself."

Alex jotted the detail down and looked up at her to ask, "And who is the beneficiary?"

Without a hint of emotion, she answered, "I am."

Alex said nothing but simply stared at her in that way he used to make people he was questioning uncomfortable enough to continue speaking. It worked like a charm on Eliza, who quickly added, "I hope you don't think that would ever make me want to kill my husband. And just in case it does, I should tell you that my husband made far more than a million dollars a year alive."

I sensed her claim surprised him as much as it did me. While Morrow's Jewelers had a wonderful reputation in Sunset Ridge, I couldn't say that the place was teeming with customers on most days of the week. Then again, jewelry had a tendency to be a high ticket item, so maybe it wasn't the quantity of customers that helped him make that much.

Whatever Alex thought of her statement, he said nothing. Instead, I saw out of the corner of my eye he wrote a note about finding Samuel and Eliza's bank accounts.

Taking the opportunity, I asked, "Mrs. Morrow, do you know anything about the day-to-day running of the jewelry store?"

My question seemed to catch her off guard, and she immediately answered, "No. Samuel took care of everything at the store. I haven't been in there for years."

She quickly followed up with, "I hope you under-stand, but this is a very difficult time for me. I have my husband's funeral to plan, so please excuse me."

Alex stood up at her cue. "I understand, Mrs. Morrow. I want to speak to your driver anyway, so now seems like the appropriate time to leave. Once we have more information on who did this terrible crime, we'll be in touch again."

A look of concern in her eyes made me wonder why she'd be bothered that we wanted to speak to Bruno. She didn't say anything against the idea, but she was clearly uncomfortable with us talking to him. But she couldn't very well say no without looking suspicious.

Just before we left, Alex asked, "Oh, Mrs. Morrow.

One last question. Did your husband have a cell phone? We didn't find one at the store."

With a tiny smile, she said, "No. My husband never thought he needed one."

We found the driver outside tending to the Mercedes. Crouching down, he sprayed cleaner on the tires just as we walked up to him.

"Hello, Bruno Carter? I'm Officer Alex Montero and this is my partner Poppy McGuire. We'd like to ask you some questions in regard to the investigation into Samuel Morrow's murder yesterday."

The man reacted to Alex's announcement by looking up at us with a blank stare and then standing up. At his full size, he proved my estimation vastly incorrect, towering over Alex by at least four inches and me by nearly a foot. I had to crane my neck to make eye contact with him.

"I don't know anything about that. I'm just the driver," he said in a deep voice that had a sort of dopey sound to it.

Alex slowly removed his pad and pen from his shirt pocket and flipped the pages until he got to the notes for the current investigation. Looking up at Bruno, he asked, "Well, what time did you leave to take her to D.C. yesterday?"

"Eight. Do you mind if I continue cleaning these tires? If you leave the stuff on too long, it's a bear to get off," Bruno asked as he crouched down to return to his task, not even bothering to wait for Alex's answer.

My partner turned to give me a look that told me he didn't appreciate this driver's lack of respect for the police and then continued with his questions. "Where did you go in D.C. and what time did you arrive there?"

Bruno thought about the answer for a second while he scrubbed the cloth over the Mercedes' right front tire and then looked up at us. "We got to Georgetown at ten."

Alex instantly jumped on his claim. "Why did it take so long since that drive should only take just over an hour?"

"There was an accident on the George Washington Parkway that tied us up for nearly forty-five minutes. You can check with the police. It was a huge accident between two tractor trailers and a bus."

"We will, thank you. Now what did you two do all day since she didn't get home until after five last night?" Alex asked.

"I don't pry into my employer's business, so I have no idea what she did. I dropped her off at the Georgetown University library at ten and picked her up when she called me at around 3:30. And if you're going to ask what took us so long to get here, it was rush hour and the city was mobbed. Something to do with a presidential motorcade or something like that. You can check it all out."

While Alex jotted the details down, I asked, "What did you do all day while Mrs. Morrow was busy at Georgetown?"

"I caught a double feature of Planet of the Apes and Beneath the Planet of the Apes at the Royale in Penn Quarter. The originals, not the new ones with all the CG. It's easy to prove. All you have to do is call them and they'll tell you the movies that were playing."

Bruno sure was a real film aficionado.

Alex snapped his notebook shut. "But that doesn't prove you were anywhere near that theater. Thank you,

Mr. Carter. If we have any other questions, we know where to find you."

With that, he turned on his heels and we walked down the driveway to the street. Once we reached the car, I said, "He wasn't helpful at all, was he?"

Nodding, Alex looked back at the driveway where Bruno remained cleaning his employer's tires. "He's certainly big enough to fracture a man's larynx, wouldn't you say?"

I didn't have to think about that answer. Bruno Carter was big enough to fracture the side of a house. One man's larynx probably wouldn't even make him break a sweat.

"I'd say so. Are you thinking he and the widow were having an affair?" I asked as we opened our doors to get into the police cruiser.

Alex slid behind the wheel and shut the driver's side door. Turning to face me, he said, "I don't know. They're one of the oddest couples I've ever seen if they are. I have a feeling the gossips will know, though, so I think it's time to go visit them."

Oh goodie. Another visit with the hens of Sunset Ridge. And I knew exactly where to find them at this time of year.

"Then just point yourself toward the former first lady's house on the next block. I imagine you should be able to catch them all there discussing the Founders' Day plans right after church."

He put the car in gear and began driving toward the Gerards' house. As we rode there, I couldn't help but notice the irony of how willing they'd be to discuss a fellow citizen's private business right after leaving church services.

That would have been lost on them, though.

Chapter Seven

THE GIRARD HOUSE loomed in front of us as we approached the front door of the former mayor and first lady's grand home. The same size as any of the others in Victorian Row, it stood out because of its bright pomegranate red exterior and jade green painted trim and shutters. For years, people had whispered behind Mrs. Girard's back about it, calling the house the Christmas Mess.

Alex looked up at the home and shook his head. "The Girards obviously don't know the meaning of the word subtle."

"And they have no sense of what looks good either. I'd guess they spent ten thousand dollars on getting the house painted these awful colors, you know that?" I said in return.

"I guess it shouldn't surprise anyone. It's not like that red hair Mrs. Girard wears is in any way natural or appealing. Every time I see it, all I can think of is she looks like a clown. You'd think one of those women she spends so much time with would tell her how bad it looks."

We stepped up onto the wrap-around porch painted jade green, and Alex rang the doorbell. "You know they talk about her behind her back and make fun of that hair," I said, feeling a twinge of pity for the former first lady.

"That wouldn't surprise me since they talk about everyone else in town. What would make any one of them exempt from their gossip?"

I knew how much he disliked meeting with these women, but every so often on a case, they could be helpful because even though neither of us approved of their backbiting and petty gossiping, we couldn't deny that they seemed to know things others in town didn't. That probably came from sitting around all day and watching their fellow citizens instead of accomplishing anything on their own.

Clearly, my opinion on the gossip coffee klatch hadn't sweetened any, despite their overwhelming approval of my life choices with Alex. That they liked my selection of a husband didn't change the fact that I thought much of what they did in Sunset Ridge hurt people needlessly.

Eileen Matthews answered the door and smiled from behind the screen door that separated us from her. Flipping her mousy brown hair off her shoulder, she said, "This is a surprise. What are you two doing here at the First Lady's home this morning? Poppy, are you here to get details on the Founders' Day plans for your article this year?"

I shook my head but didn't tell Eileen that I didn't need any more details about the event since it never really changed from year to year and Howard didn't want anything more than the piece I'd always written. Instead, I gave her question a shrug and said, "Maybe next week. Today, Alex and I would like to speak to you ladies and hopefully benefit from your extensive knowledge of Sunset Ridge."

In the past three years, Eileen had slowly grown to be as obnoxious as the rest of the biddies in the Founders' Day Committee, so by now I didn't see her as any different than them. As disappointing as that was, it did make it easier dealing with them en masse since all I had to do was be ingratiating to the point of being sickening. My pride suffered a little, but whatever I needed to do with them invariably became easier.

Her ego stroked, she eagerly opened the door and welcomed us into the Girard house. In all my time in Sunset Ridge, I'd never been inside their home. Although I had expected the décor to match the outside of the home, even that hadn't prepared me for how garishly they had decorated the interior.

Everywhere my gaze fell I saw knickknacks. The place looked like a museum for useless junk. A set of tiny figurines of frogs with guitars on lily pads lined the top of a fireplace, as if they were items to be shown off to visitors as they entered the home. Decorative tea cups from the size of a thimble to one that looked like it could be used as an aquarium in a pinch sat around on end tables and shelves, none of them looking like they matched anything else in the room.

And those were just the small things about the room we stood in. The furniture looked to be straight out of the actual Victorian period, but none of the pieces would be truly considered antiques anyone would want. A couch upholstered in a multicolor tapestry depicting what looked like some medieval battle made me cringe at the thought that some misguided soul at some point in time had actually wanted to sit on something that mimicked the Bayeux Tapestry.

Even worse was the reality that the Girards had paid for that piece, probably handsomely, and thought the couch should be displayed so anyone visiting their home would see it.

Nearby, a high backed chair that looked to be in deep blue velvet and came up over the head of the person sitting in it resembled a partial Iron Maiden more than anything else. I had to look away, but everywhere around me existed another decorating tragedy.

Some things went out of style for a reason.

Alex leaned in as we followed Eileen to another room and whispered, "Damn, this place is like a house of horrors."

A shiver of disgust overtook me, and I simply nodded, not able to say anything in response. House of horrors indeed.

We walked through a doorway to a smaller sitting room decorated just slightly less grotesquely. This room had been painted the exact shade of green used in the felt on pool tables. This gave it the effect of the ten foot high walls closing in on you as soon as you stepped into it.

Definitely not the kind of place I'd want to spend any considerable time. Silently, I prayed the ladies gave us what we needed quickly so we could escape this place in a hurry.

"Ladies, look who came to visit us today," Eileen announced before taking her seat in an old style burgundy velvet chair with gilded trim that matched the other three her friends sat in around a large wood table with nail heads around the top edge.

Mrs. Scanlon's grey eyes lit up at the sight of the two

of us standing there. "Poppy and Officer Montero! What a wonderful surprise! And so close to your big day. Is everything ready? You know you don't want to wait until the last minute."

I felt Alex tense up next to me at hearing yet another person he barely knew interjecting themselves into our wedding plans with their opinion. Happy to take the lead in this part of our visit, I put on my cutest smile for her and said, "Oh, I know it, but everything's ready. All we need to do is get the two of us to the church."

Eileen smiled and pointed us to a tan couch that seemed to match nothing in the room and certainly didn't feel like it fit with anything Victorian. "I'm sure that won't be a problem then. It's going to be a lovely wedding, I'm sure."

We sat down as I heard her say for the second time how sure she was about our wedding plans. Dangerously close to having the old maid moniker tacked onto her, she seemed a little too happy when she spoke about our big day.

I took Alex's hand in mine and gave it a squeeze. "As long as this guy is there with me, it's going to be the happiest day of my life," I cooed.

My almost sickeningly sweet tone made him look at me strangely, but I knew what worked with these women. Eleanor Girard tilted her chin up and gazed down her nose to study the two of us for a moment before adding her own comment about our big day.

"You've found a very nice one in him, Poppy," she said with that pompous air she liked to affect, referring to one of the town's police officers in a way that made it sound like I'd chosen a good horse.

His fingers squeezed mine in a signal that told me he

wanted to get on with our business there and end this discussion of us as a couple and our wedding plans, so I thanked her politely.

"Thank you. I agree, Mrs. Girard."

The pleasantries finished, Alex jumped right in with his questions. "Ladies, we're here because we're investigating the death of Samuel Morrow. I'm sure you've heard by now that he was found murdered in his store yesterday morning. We're hoping you might know something that could help the police find his killer."

The Widow Dunn made a sound of disapproval and shook her head. "Tsk, tsk. I did hear that, and it's quite a shame. Samuel Morrow was a proper jeweler and not like those flim flam artists at the malls. He knew the value of a fine piece of jewelry just by looking at it. I can tell you that."

I couldn't decide which bothered her—Samuel's death or the fact that he wouldn't be around to appraise her jewelry anymore.

"I was so sorry to hear of his death," Mrs. Scanlon said, shaking her head slowly so her chin length grey hairdo swung in slow motion. "He was the kind of man this town needs."

Feeling like they needed some egging on, I quickly asked, "Even though he rarely participated in town events?"

The four women nodded in unison, and the former first lady came to his defense. "He worked day and night in that store of his. It wasn't his responsibility to participate. He did what was expected of him in this town. His wife, on the other hand, the same can't be said for her."

And there it was. Our in to get the gossips talking

about Eliza Morrow.

The nodding intensified at the mention of Eliza's lack of real participation in the town's events. I'd suspected the gossips disapproved of her not giving her all for things like Founders' Day or the Christmas decorating festival. Now we just had to listen to what they had to say.

"Do you know I saw her last month as she was leaving her house and she didn't even acknowledge my hello?" the Widow Dunn huffed. "She intentionally avoided me, and I bet I know why. She knows Founders' Day is right around the corner, and once again, she won't lift a single finger to help. Oh, we'll get a check all right, but you won't see her on Main Street for not one moment of the most important event of the year for Sunset Ridge."

"She thinks money is enough," Mrs. Scanlon said in a tone full of disgust and disapproval. "That's how you know she's new money."

Alex glanced over at me at the mention of new money. We both knew once the town gossips trotted out the new money insult that things would soon get vicious.

But I wanted to help them along so we didn't get stuck listening to them bash Eliza Morrow for the rest of the day, so I said, "She and Samuel had been married for twenty-five years, though. Can that still be considered new money?"

I knew the answer before I even asked the question. Yes, it could be. New money wasn't determined by time so much as attitude and behavior.

"Oh yes!" the former First Lady said with all the attitude she could muster. "That money was always Samuel's. She never made one red cent of it. All she ever did was ride around in that silver Mercedes of hers, not even waving hello when she saw any of her fellow citizens."

Before Alex or I could say a word, Eileen Matthews jumped in and began piling on. "And speaking of her riding around in that car, what is going on with that driver of hers? What is he, like twenty-five? Why would a married woman in her late forties have a man like that driving her everywhere? Doesn't she know how bad that looks?"

"She doesn't care," the Widow Dunn said in her nastiest voice. "I heard there were problems in that marriage, and if that was the case, it's no wonder. No man who spends hours upon hours slaving away to make a successful business like Morrow's Jewelers to provide his wife with a house like she has wants to see his wife being driven around with some beef hunk."

Beef hunk? I didn't even want to ask her to clarify what she meant by that.

"Beefcake," Eileen corrected her. "I think he'd be called beefcake."

The Widow Dunn looked at her and grimaced in disgust before snapping, "I don't care what he'd be called. It's not right. Everyone in town knows it too. She looks ridiculous having him drive her around, and it made Samuel look like a fool."

Alex nudged my knee with his, so I jumped at the chance to get the ladies to talk about more salacious topics related to Eliza Morrow. "Do you really think there's something between her and her driver?"

One after another, the women nodded and said, "Yes."

Mrs. Scanlon then added, "I heard that Samuel

hired a private detective because he thought something untoward was going on too."

For the first time since they started bashing Eliza, Alex spoke up. "When, Mrs. Scanlon? Do you know when Samuel was supposed to have hired this person?"

She didn't answer for a moment and looked surprised to hear him join the conversation, but then she said, "I heard that right around Easter this year."

"Do you remember who told you that?" he asked, unknowingly breaking the gossips' code.

Who said it didn't matter as much as what they said. Well, unless the person gossiping said something that reflected on them personally. Then who was doing the talking meant a great deal. But even then, they didn't share their sources.

Not even with a policeman they liked.

I quickly worked to repair the damage of Alex's unfortunate faux pas. "So Samuel actually suspected something was going on with his wife and the driver? Do you think he ever found any evidence to prove it?" I asked eagerly, as if I felt the same way as the four women did about the situation.

Mrs. Scanlon sighed but I thankfully saw my questions distracted her from what Alex had interjected into the conversation. "I don't know, but I wouldn't be surprised to find out he did. I mean, look at the way she acts as if that whole Driving Miss Daisy thing she's doing with that young man isn't going to make people talk."

"If I were her husband, I would have been doing some checking up on her. Samuel spent every day working to make that store a success, and what did he get for it? A wife who didn't understand her responsibilities to him or this town. It just burns me up as someone who's devoted her life to our beautiful town," Mrs. Girard preached, surprisingly not going into chapter and verse about all that she'd done as the first lady of Sunset Ridge.

Mrs. Scanlon and Eileen Matthews both patted her arms in solidarity for her tireless efforts to make our town the best it could be. Alex nudged my knee again, and I looked to my right to see his eyes glazing over. Males never understood how these kinds of conversations could go on for so long. I knew he had gotten something he thought he could use and wanted to flee from that room and those women, but I had a sense they might be able to give us something even more.

"It's such a shame about Samuel. Can you imagine anyone wanting to hurt such a sweet man?" I asked as I frowned and shook my head, mimicking the four women in front of me.

They all agreed that it was terribly shocking, and Eileen Matthews asked, "Did Samuel have any enemies? I have such a hard time imagining anyone wanting to hurt that dear man."

Her question was met with silence for a few moments, giving Alex the cue that it was time for us to leave, but as he moved to leave, Mrs. Scanlon quietly said, "Not to speak ill of the dead, but I can only imagine how upset Ralph Martin was when Samuel put up that new sign of his that juts out so far that it hides the Martin's Pharmacy sign. You can't even see Ralph's sign when you're driving up Main Street coming from the south. I'm sure it's hurt his business."

Alex sat down again as she spoke, and when she finished, he and I looked at each other wide-eyed. I would have never given a single thought to the idea of hard feelings between Samuel and Ralph Martin over a sign. I had feeling by the look of surprise on Alex's face that he wouldn't have either.

"That's incredible, Mrs. Scanlon," I said, honestly complimenting her. "I never thought of that, but you're right. You can't even see the Martin's Pharmacy sign when you're driving up from the police station. I never realized that until right now."

She beamed at my words but gave credit where it was truly due. "Mr. Scanlon noticed it, actually, and as soon as he pointed it out to me, I said to him, 'That's going to cause a problem for poor Ralph Martin' and he agreed."

Alex gave me a look that told me he'd heard enough and needed to get out of there before he began to speak his mind. The last thing we needed was the town gossips working against him and his official efforts, so I nodded and stood from the couch when he did.

"We have to go, but thank you so much for all your help, ladies. We appreciate you taking the time to help us today," Alex said in his best respectful tone.

"Oh, it's our pleasure," Mrs. Scanlon cooed, still happy that I'd said such nice things about her ability to see things neither Alex nor I had.

"We all look forward to your reception, you two," Eileen said as she stood up to escort us out. "I just know it's going to be a beautiful day."

"Thank you, Eileen," I said, suddenly feeling bad for what I thought about her earlier.

She walked us to the front door, and after Alex thanked her again and said goodbye, she took me into her arms in a hug I hadn't expected. I returned the embrace, surprised at her sudden show of affection. She had always said I was one of her favorite students, though.

Then just before I walked out, she whispered in a low voice, "I was meaning to ask you something, Poppy. I know you probably sat me with the ladies in there, but would it be possible to seat me at another table with other people at the reception? It's hard, I know, because I'm attending alone, but I'd really appreciate it if you could. I'm okay even if you put me with cousins you don't even like."

I nodded and smiled. "I can handle that for you. Are you sure it won't be a problem with the ladies in there?"

She shrugged at my question. "I'm not worried."

Maybe Eileen hadn't changed as much as I thought. Maybe there was hope for her after all. I had a nice middle-aged cousin who had RSVP'd that he was coming to the wedding alone. Perhaps seating her next to him at the reception would be a good thing for both of them.

At the very least, it would be getting her away from the town gossips for a few hours.

The romantic in me liked that idea a lot. It would mean rearranging the tables a little, something I didn't relish doing just a few weeks out, but for romance, it would be worth it.

Chapter Eight

WE HEADED INTO the police station with a host of questions to seek answers for. Had Samuel hired a private investigator to follow his wife? And if he had, was it because he suspected her of being unfaithful? And what about that sign he put up at the end of last winter? Had it caused a rift between him and Ralph Martin?

More than anything else, did either of these possibilities come anywhere close to making someone want to kill Samuel Morrow? And if so, why did the murderer take my wedding band from the jewelry store?

Neither Alex nor I had mentioned the missing ring when we questioned Eliza, her beefcake driver, or the Founders' Day committee ladies. For my part, I hadn't said anything because I'd grown to loathe questions about the wedding and all the plans that surrounded it. I hadn't asked Alex why he never brought it up to any of the people we'd spoken to, but I suspected it had more to do with keeping that part of the case under wraps for now than not wanting to discuss how his soon-to-be bride wouldn't have a wedding band for him to slip on her finger on the big day.

And that said something since every time anyone in town even began to broach the subject of our wedding, he cringed. More than anything else, Alex Montero was a private man. That he happened to be marrying me made safeguarding that privacy a Herculean task, for sure.

"Poppy, I'm going to get working on getting Samuel's bank, credit card, and phone records. Since he didn't use a cell, we only have to get a hold of the store's phone records and the house phone records, for now."

"But what if that's in his wife's name?" I asked, suspecting nothing was in Eliza Morrow's name.

Alex smirked. "I have a feeling everything was in our victim's name. She hasn't worked since they moved here over twenty years ago. I'd bet the utilities, credit cards, and the mortgage were all in his name."

I nodded, but the setup all sounded so old fashioned. Maybe I'd been single for too long, but the thought of everything in my world being in my husband's name sounded completely foreign.

As he worked the phone to get Samuel's bank and phone records, I mulled over our interview with Eliza Morrow. I'd thought of her as severe, but as she spoke to us sitting in that beautifully decorated living room, at times she'd been downright icy. I wanted to give her the benefit of the doubt since I knew as well as anyone that mourning was an intensely individual matter. The problem was that nothing in her behavior said she was mourning.

And how likely was her claim that she hadn't been inside her husband's jewelry store in years? I tried to imagine my husband's business being less than half a mile from my home and never once stopping in over the years, and it seemed improbable. Had she said that just to make sure we didn't think she could be the murderer?

If so, it had backfired.

Then again, Eliza had rarely been seen walking anywhere in town, so perhaps as Bruno Carter drove her out of town each time, likely passing right by Morrow's Jewelry, she never told him to stop so she could pay a visit to her husband. Perhaps she and Samuel preferred to keep his business life and their personal life separate.

That I could certainly understand.

And what about that driver, Bruno, who looked like a model and had a body that made me think he spent hours each day at the gym? Who was this guy and why was he driving a woman twenty years his senior around? While it seemed to be a full-time job for him, he couldn't be making good money being a driver and resident car washer.

And speaking of being a resident, did he live at the Morrow's too? If not, did he live nearby and walk to his work as a driver? That would be strange, at the very least.

I wished I knew how Samuel had felt about his wife's driver. Unfortunately, we'd never been that close, so we'd never spoken about anything other than jewelry or small talk in passing about the weather and other pleasantries. Now that he was gone, I regretted not making more of an effort.

Was it possible that he suspected his wife of having an affair? I didn't think she and the beefcake were sneaking around behind his back, but something seemed off about that guy. He seemed too protective of her and not like he cared at all about Samuel Morrow being murdered.

Alex got off the phone and turned to look at me. "You look a million miles away right now. What's on your mind?"

"Eliza and her driver."

"And what do you think?" he asked, cocking one eyebrow and smiling like he was amused by something.

"I'm not sure. All I know is my gut is telling me something's off with them. I don't know what, though."

"Do you think Mrs. Morrow was having an affair?"

I thought about it for a moment before answering, "I don't know. If so, they make one of the oddest looking couples I've ever seen. I'm having a hard time picturing them together."

He chuckled at me. "I find it better, overall, not to picture most people together."

"Well, I'm not sure about them cheating. All I know is I had a sure sense something was off between them."

"I trust your gut, Poppy, so I'm not ruling anything out yet."

"Thanks," I said, beaming a smile.

Nodding, he leaned back in his chair and folded his arms across his chest. "Hopefully we won't have to wait too long to get a look at those phone and bank records. If Samuel was having a private investigator watch his wife, we'll be able to see that somewhere in them."

"Until then, what are we going to do?" I asked, antsy to get really moving on this case.

He thought about my question for a moment and sat forward in his chair. "I'll tell you what. Since you look like you're about to jump out of that seat, how about you take a walk up to Martin's Pharmacy and strike up a conversation with Ralph Martin? See if Mrs. Scanlon is onto anything with that idea of hers that Samuel's sign was a thorn in Ralph's side."

I jumped up from my chair, thrilled to not only get

out of his office but also that Alex trusted me enough to let me go interview someone for the case. It wouldn't be anything official and wouldn't hold up in court, but I wasn't going to be trying to extract a confession from Ralph Martin. Alex wanted my sense of how he felt about Samuel and his sign, and that made me feel more valuable than I ever had on any case we'd worked together.

"Okay! I'll take a walk up there and see what I can find out. Maybe we can grab a bite to eat when I get back," I said as I headed toward the door.

"Oh, yeah. That sounds fine. I didn't expect you to run out like this, but I'm happy that you're enthusiastic about going to talk to him. Just be careful."

I spun on my heels and smiled at Alex. "Not that I'm trying to get away from you or anything, but this is the first time you've ever had me do anything like this on a case. So I'm pretty excited about it. And it's broad daylight, so I think I'll be fine walking up the street."

As usual, Alex showed his cautious side and held his hands up to slow me down. "Don't get crazy with this, Poppy. Remember, you aren't officially a cop. You're just a deputy. I'm not even sure if he says anything to you that it would be admissible in court. I just trust your gut enough that I want to know what you think Ralph is feeling about Samuel's death."

"It means a lot to me that you think my gut is trustworthy, Alex. I won't let you down."

I made a move to leave but heard him say, "I love you, Poppy."

Looking back at him, I blew him a kiss. "I love you. See you in a little while."

Happy to go out and do field work on my own, I

headed out of the station and up Main Street toward Martin's Pharmacy. As I walked up the street, I noticed the flower baskets hanging from the lampposts that the Founders' Day committee had planned to put up in advance of the events next month. I had to admit that those ladies sure did good things for the town, even if the price we all paid was having them lord over everyone with their gossip.

The pink, yellow, and white flowers in the baskets made me even happier, so by the time I reached Ralph Martin's pharmacy, I had to remember to dial back my joy since I was about to speak to him about the death of his business neighbor. It wouldn't do to be discussing poor Samuel's demise with a silly smile on my face.

Martin's Pharmacy felt like someone had frozen it in time and protected it from much of modern day America. Unlike major chain pharmacies, Martin's didn't carry much more than drugs and medical supplies. A few grocery items, but no makeup or seasonal goods like rakes, shovels, or sand pails made their way onto the shelves of the store.

No, like drug stores of old, Martin's offered any kind of over the counter medicine for headaches to back pain, along with ACE bandages in a variety of sizes and a selection of canes that couldn't be found anywhere else in Sunset Ridge. And behind the counter of the pharmacy, Ralph filled any prescription you handed him.

He carried greeting cards for a while when I was a little girl until Gladys McMullen opened her stationery shop called The Write Way at the other end of Main Street. Shortly after at a town council meeting, they came to an agreement that she wouldn't carry anything that could be considered medicinal and he wouldn't sell cards so as not to intrude on her business. Since then, any time anyone asked about greeting cards, Ralph happily pointed them down the street to The Write Way and told them to say hi to Gladys. In return, she dropped the Martin Pharmacy name in any conversation she could in her shop.

I walked toward Ralph's store and looked up at Samuel's sign hanging over the sidewalk. Just as Mrs. Scanlon had said, I couldn't see the much smaller Martin Pharmacy sign behind it. I stopped in front of the business and looked in through the windows. Just like it always looked, the walls were painted a pristine white, and the fluorescent lights lined the ceiling, illuminating the store.

The bell on top of the front door jingled as walked in to see if I could speak to the owner himself. Rows of white metal shelves to the left and right of a main aisle stood meticulously stocked and ready for any physical malady customers might have. A handful of customers milled about checking labels and tossing their chosen purchases into the metal baskets they held in their hands. At the far end of the store up on a level about three feet higher than the rest of the store a half wall painted white to match everything else separated Ralph and the pharmacy section from the floor below.

I craned my neck to see him standing behind the wall, the top of his head the only part of him showing. He hummed the tune playing low on the store's speakers, a Muzak version of Donna Summer's She Works Hard For The Money, as his thin hair bounced to the tune. I chuckled at the image of him dancing his heart out to an eighties tune behind that wall.

"Mr. Martin? Do you have a minute to talk?" I called out loud enough so he could hear me.

He immediately poked his head around the end of the half wall and smiled warmly at me. "Poppy McGuire, the soon-to-be bride! What can I do for you today?"

At that moment, I realized I hadn't thought of any cover story for my visit, so I quickly scrambled to come up with something believable. "I was wondering if you had anything to brighten my teeth a little. I've always thought they were just fine, but next to my wedding dress, I feel like I look like some backwoodsman who's spent the last ten years chewing tobacco."

Ralph walked around the wall and came down to stand behind the register sitting on the glass case in front of me. "That's crazy. You have a gorgeous smile, Poppy, but if you really want to brighten up your teeth a little, look in aisle three. I hear customers like the strips the best."

He pointed in the direction where the toothpaste was displayed, and I pretended to pay attention to where I could find what he suggested. After looking over at aisle three, I turned back to face him and nodded.

"Thanks, Mr. Martin. How have you been? I haven't seen you in a few weeks."

"Well, I've been good. Thank you for asking, Poppy," he said with a broad smile before catching himself and forcing a serious expression onto his face. "That is until yesterday. I'm still in shock."

I nodded again to let him know I shared in his disbelief at what had happened to Samuel. "It is so terrible. It's almost too much to think about. Samuel was such a wonderful man."

"He was. This town will miss him."

I watched as Ralph spoke about his next door neighbor in the business district and spotted no hints of pleasure that Samuel had been killed and no trace of anything resembling resentment toward him. He appeared to be genuinely unhappy that the jeweler had been killed.

However, I pressed on, knowing that even the most ordinary of people could successfully pretend to be something they weren't.

"Were the two of you close, Mr. Martin?" I asked, keenly focused on his face for any changes in his expression when he heard my question.

But he simply nodded and smiled. "I think we were. Samuel Morrow was a true businessman in every sense of the word, and that included how he interacted with the rest of us here on Main Street."

"What do you mean?"

"Not many people know this, but whenever Samuel planned on having a special sale in his store, he always approached every other store owner on the street to ask if they wanted to participate in some way. He sold the most profitable merchandise in town, yet he never failed to include everyone else in his success. That kind of professionalism isn't as common as it should be."

I'd never heard that about Samuel, but it didn't surprise me. His goodness came through loud and clear every time you entered his store or saw him on the street.

"So you weren't upset when he put that big sign up in front of his store that blocks yours?"

Ralph chuckled and waved away even the suggestion of his being angry at Samuel. "No. You should have seen his face when the sign company came to put it up. His eyes practically bugged right out of his head as he stood there and watched them hang that sign. I didn't even get a chance to come out and see it before he came running into the store to tell me how it was all a big mistake and he'd fix it. The replacement sign was scheduled to come at the beginning of June."

He began to choke up on his words and sighed. "I can't believe someone could do that to him, Poppy. I know you've been working with the police. Do they have any idea who did it?"

Not wanting to share any details I knew weren't for public consumption yet, I simply shook my head and frowned. "It's early yet, but I know they're working very hard to solve this case. Samuel was loved by everyone in town."

"That he was. As I told the officer who came by that day, I have a hard time imagining anyone from Sunset Ridge could have done that to him," Ralph said sadly.

"We spoke to his wife this morning. I can't imagine how hard it is to lose your husband after twenty-five years."

For a moment, he just nodded without saying a word, but I had a feeling there something was behind his silence. I waited a few moments more for him to continue the conversation and watched as he opened his mouth to speak and then closed his lips tightly, as if to stop the words from accidentally flying out.

Wanting to encourage him to say what was on his mind, I said, "She seems very strong, at least from what I saw when we spoke to her today. I can only hope that I'd be that strong if something happened to Alex."

That loosened Ralph's tongue, and after he twisted

his face into an expression of distaste, he quietly said, "There's strength, and then there's strength. Some is better than others."

I wanted to hear more about his ideas about strength, specifically Eliza Morrow's brand of strength, but a customer interrupted us with a question about a prescription she held in her hand for a cream to help her eczema. The painfully thin woman stared at Ralph with wide eyes like he was the savior she'd been waiting all her life for to solve her problem, so I figured I wouldn't be able to get any more from him and excused myself so she could have his complete attention. She elbowed me out of the way once she got the signal that our conversation had come to an end, and I turned and left the store still wondering what Ralph had meant by that comment about strength.

"Hey, Poppy! How are you?" a man's voice called out as I started on my way back to report what I'd found out to Alex.

I turned around to see Nate Cardow standing outside his shoe store smiling at me. A sweet man of around fifty, he'd known my father for years and always treated me like the daughter he never had. He liked to wear sweater vests that only served to accentuate the roundness of his middle-aged belly years of drinking beer at McGuire's has created.

"Hi Nate! How are you today?"

He began to walk toward me, still smiling like seeing me made his day. "I'm better now. It's so nice to see you. Were you getting a prescription filled at Ralph's?"

"No. I was just taking a walk on this beautiful May day. I'm just heading back to the station."

"You're still working with the police on cases? I

know your father worries himself sick about that. Maybe you should take a break from it for a while."

Clearly, my father had been doing some talking behind the bar. I knew he worried, but did he have to tell all his buddies about it? They were worse than the town gossips sometimes.

I patted Nate on the shoulder and chuckled. "I love it, though, so my father is going to have to keep worrying and trust that Alex won't let anything happen to his soon-to-be bride. Nice seeing you again! Have a great one!"

I left him standing there in front of his store and made my way back down Main Street toward the police station feeling like I'd accomplished something in my time with Ralph. Mrs. Scanlon had seemed to misconstrue how he'd felt about that oversized sign of Samuel's. That didn't really surprise me, though. She was always trying to stir up trouble wherever she could, and creating problems between a dead man and a fellow businessman certainly wasn't the worst thing she'd ever done with her gossip.

By the time I reached Alex's office, I had rehearsed my report on what had transpired at Martin's Pharmacy at least three times. I knew it wasn't a big deal or anything like that, but for the first time speaking to a person on a case alone, I wanted to get it right.

Alex sat typing on his laptop when I walked in, and he looked up with anticipation in his eyes when he saw I'd returned. "Back so soon? Did you find out anything?"

"You doubt me?" I joked as I sat down in front of his desk.

Shaking his head, he smiled. "Never. I've seen your

talent in getting people to talk, Poppy. It's practically supernatural. You could go into a room with ten perfect strangers and come out an hour later with all their deepest, darkest secrets."

"Oh, stop," I said, outwardly dismissing his compliments while inside I loved hearing them.

When he didn't say anything more, I joked, "Well, I guess you took me seriously. But feel free any time to stroke my ego like that again. So I found out that Ralph wasn't bothered in the least about that sign of Samuel's."

Alex looked disappointed by my announcement. Frowning, he said, "Oh. Okay. I guess Mrs. Scanlon was wrong."

"She sure was. Ralph told me that he never even had a chance to say anything to Samuel before he apologized for the sign's size. I guess it was a mistake, and a new one is being made to replace it. It's supposed to be switched out early next month. Or at least it was supposed to. So the whole sign thing was a dead end."

"I had a feeling it might be. Oh well. Thanks for checking that out."

He began to tap away on his laptop again, but I cleared my throat and he looked across the desk at me, clearly confused. "Something else you want to talk about?"

I'd practiced this whole report the whole way down Main Street, and now he'd pretty much ruined all I'd planned. Disappointed, I said, "Yes. I didn't spend my entire time talking about that silly giant sign, you know."

Alex swiveled in his office chair so he faced me directly and gave me his undivided attention. "I'm sorry. I'm a little distracted. What else did you find out?"

"Well, I let Ralph know that we had spoken to Eliza

Morrow earlier today, and he said something very interesting when I told him that I thought she was strong in how she was handling the death of her husband."

Leaning forward, he asked, "Something interesting? Like what?"

I smiled and repeated Ralph's words exactly as he'd said them to me. "He said, 'There's strength, and then there's strength. Some is better than others.'"

Alex's eyebrows slowly raised up into his forehead. "He said that about Eliza Morrow?"

"Yep."

"Did he say anything else?" Alex asked, clearly interested in what I had to report.

I shook my head, wishing I had more to tell him. If only that pencil thin woman hadn't interrupted us, I might have kept him talking a bit longer.

"No. One of his customers needed him to help her with her eczema prescription, so I didn't have a chance to get any more out of him. But I thought that comment all on its own was pretty interesting."

"It certainly isn't a ringing endorsement of Eliza Morrow as a sympathetic figure," Alex said, sitting back in his chair.

"I have the feeling very few people would say a lot nice about her. Being standoffish in a small town usually puts people off, and Eliza Morrow is the definition of standoffish."

"I wonder what he meant," Alex said, echoing the very thought in my mind at that moment.

"No idea, but I thought you'd find it interesting. Did you find out anything from the financial and phone records yet?"

He shook his head. "Not yet. We got the judge to

sign off on us getting them, but it's Sunday so it might take a little longer."

Surprised to hear he'd made so much progress in the short time I'd been gone, I said, "You got Judge Harlow to do work on a Sunday? I'm impressed."

Alex threw his head back and laughed. "You'd be amazed how helpful he is on Sundays. I think it's the only day he doesn't drink, so other than the hangover early in the morning, he's pretty useful. Thank God, right, or we wouldn't get anything on those records until tomorrow."

"Speaking of tomorrow, we have the cake tasting," I reminded him. "You didn't forget, did you?"

He cringed, narrowing his eyes to slits. "No, but I'm still confused as to why we have to taste anything. It's wedding cake. I've been to dozens of weddings, and every single piece of wedding cake has tasted the same. Tasteless cake with too sweet icing. It's like there's a universal recipe every baker knows."

Alex had given me a hassle about this cake tasting idea ever since I first brought it up. He simply didn't understand that a wedding cake didn't have to be that awful dessert that tasted like sawdust and pure sugar topping.

"We have to taste samples so we know what we want our cake to taste like so it doesn't taste like that typical wedding cake. I made sure to tell the lady at Charming that your favorite cake flavor is chocolate and mine is spice, so I expect those two will be part of the tasting. And I've told her that neither one of us like that stiff icing that makes you feel like your teeth are rotting out of your head, so there won't be any of that."

"Well, that's good."

"And I want fresh flowers on the cake, so she knows that."

He squinted again, but this time he looked confused. "Fresh flowers? Are people going to be eating real flowers? I'm not sure I'm up for that, although my grandmother made dandelion wine years ago that my friend and I got into when we were teenagers and got pretty smashed off of."

I had to laugh. Even when he was being difficult, he could still be quite cute. "Well, I'm not planning on having the flowers get anyone smashed, but don't worry. I'm sure my father will make sure the alcohol is flowing just fine. This is a half Irish wedding, after all."

"With the other half Italian, which adds to the celebrating. We'll be lucky if Sunset Ridge is the same ever again after this wedding."

I winked at him and chuckled. "I suspect it won't be, in fact. One of this town's old maids is marrying one of the most eligible bachelors in Sunset Ridge. The place is going to be forever changed after our wedding."

Alex rolled his eyes. "I leave the most eligible bachelor in town thing to Derek. He's had a lot of practice in the role. And you've never been an old maid."

Before I could say I was worried about Derek after his breakup months ago from Solange, Alex's computer made a sound to let him know he had a new email. Clicking on it, he smiled at me.

"Time to check out the bank records and see what Samuel knew or didn't know."

Chapter Nine

S TOPPING HIM, I stood up and said, "Let me go get Craig. Give me a minute."

"Okay. I'm going to print these out, so take your time."

I took an easy stroll down the hallway to Craig's desk and found him reading the Sunset Ridge Officer's Handbook. Engrossed in whatever it had to say, he didn't notice me standing in front of him, so I softly tapped on his desk.

"Hey, I didn't know you were standing there," he said, quickly closing the handbook and shoving it into his side desk drawer. "What's up?"

"Alex has Samuel's bank records, so I figured we should all be there when we start reading through them," I said with a smile as I motioned back toward his office.

Craig frowned but nodded. The effect seemed strange and awkward. "Oh. Okay. Tell him I'll be there in a minute." He stopped for a second before he stood up and said, "Forget it. I'll come right now."

I wanted to ask if something was wrong, but he walked away toward Alex's office without another word, so I followed him, wondering what was bothering him. I couldn't catch up to Craig before he walked in and began talking to Alex, but I made a mental note to be sure to find out what was on Craig's mind.

"Harlow is on a roll today," Craig said as he sat down in his usual seat in front of Alex's desk. "Josh said he got him to sign an order already today too."

"If only every day could be Sunday," I mused as I sat down next to him. "Or if we lived in a dry town. That would work too."

Alex laughed, but Craig remained stone-faced after my joke. I wasn't a comedienne by any stretch of the imagination, but my humorous comments usually at least got a smirk from most people ever since Stephen quit the force. Had something changed between Craig and me that I didn't know about? Had I offended him in some way?

I definitely needed to talk to him at some point so I could straighten out whatever was going on. What had happened with Stephen wasn't going to happen again.

Alex handed us each copies of the bank records. "I've skimmed through these already and some things jumped out at me, but I want to know what you guys think."

"You know, you could have just sent the file to the two of us and saved all this paper and ink," I teased him.

He smirked and pointed at the stack of papers in my hand. "I'm old fashioned. It's something you're supposed to love about me. Take a look and tell me what you see in them."

Surprised he'd said anything about how we felt about one another at work, I made a silly face at him and then focused my attention on the information the bank had provided. Samuel banked at Third National

Bank of Maryland, but had a number of accounts with them. The commercial account for Morrow Jewelers seemed to be pretty much straightforward with deposits each day and withdrawals for bill payments and salary payments for Samuel, the only person who worked at the store.

As I scanned the numbers, for the first time it dawned on me that Samuel ran that entire business by himself. He was the only sales employee while at the same time being the only buyer for the store.

The numbers surprised me somewhat, though. Eliza Morrow hadn't exaggerated by much when she said her husband was worth more alive than dead. Although Morrow Jewelers rarely had more than one or two customers in the store at any time I'd noticed, the business made a substantial income each month, surpassing one hundred thousand a month.

"How on earth did that business make that kind of money in this town?" I asked as I continued to peruse the bank records for the store.

"Online sales," Alex said, making me look up in surprise. "He had a website and even sold on Amazon."

"Really? I'd pegged Samuel for some small town, old fashioned shopkeeper, and here he was selling thousands each month online. Good for him."

The level of insensitivity in my words hit me as both Alex and Craig stared at me. "Well, it was good until some monster took his life. That's all I meant. I'm going to close my mouth and read through these records now."

I returned to scanning the numbers in front of me, feeling awkward about how I'd put my foot into my mouth. After a few minutes of silence, Craig spoke up and said, "What is the payment to someone named

Jefferson Sterling? It's on page eighteen from the personal account that had only his name on it. It's for five grand in January of this year. That's a lot of money, don't you think?"

As I shuffled the stack of papers I held to get to page eighteen, Alex said, "What name did you say? Jefferson Sterling? I know that name. How, though? Give me a minute. It will come to me."

I read the information on the page about this Sterling man and then flipped the page to see if any other payments were made to him from that same account. I read back as far as the records went and saw nothing more mentioned about him, so I continued into the personal account Samuel and his wife shared and saw no other entry about any payment to Sterling.

"That's the only one I can see," I said to Alex and Craig.

"One payment of five grand to him from a private account only Samuel drew on. Any chance it had something to do with the jewelry business but he just needed to use money from his personal account?" Craig asked, directing his question more toward Alex than me.

"I don't know. What I do want to know is who Jefferson Sterling is. I know that name. It's from something…" Alex said, letting his sentence trail off into silence.

"Maybe he has a website," I suggested, growing more curious by the second who this man was and why Samuel had paid him five thousand dollars at the beginning of the year.

Alex pointed at me, nodding his head enthusiastically. "That's a good idea. I might as well Google his name and see what comes up."

While he typed away to search for information on Jefferson Sterling, I walked around the desk to see what came up. As soon as Alex read the first listing—a headline from a Baltimore newspaper article—he clapped his hands together in excitement.

"I knew it! I knew I'd heard his name before and in a case too. He's a private eye in the Baltimore area."

Scanning the page, I read through the entries until his website came up near the bottom. I pointed at it. "Click on that. I want to see this guy's website. What exactly do you put on a private eye's website? Hoping to catch your significant other cheating on you with some beefcake? You've come to the right place. We'll prove she's unfaithful or your money back."

Alex looked up at me and rolled his eyes as the page loaded. "You're in rare form today, Poppy."

Before we could examine Jefferson Sterling P.I.'s site, Craig announced, "I need to go talk to Derek about something. I'll be back in a few minutes."

We looked at him, the two of us surprised as he walked out without saying another word, and then at each other. "Was it something I said?" I asked, half-joking but still worried about what could be bothering Craig.

"I don't know. I guess he had to talk to Derek about something."

"I guess so."

Focusing my attention back on the website of our P.I., I noticed whoever had made his site hadn't put much effort into it. A basic black background and some white text in Times New Roman font showed he'd either done it himself or he'd been overcharged by someone who created it for him.

"This is the lamest website I've ever seen," I said as I pointed to his name at the top of the page. "I think I feel bad for this guy."

Alex shook his head and scrolled down to where his office address was listed. "Don't. I remember where I knew him from. A case right after I joined the force. He was hired by a husband who thought his wife was cheating on him with his business partner. The man ended up murdering both of them on Sterling's report that they had been sleeping together. The guy said he wished he never found out the truth. Sterling's kind are nothing but trouble."

He jotted down the office address and closed the page as I walked toward his office door to look out into the hallway. "It's not like it was Sterling's fault anyone got killed. He was hired for a job. He didn't kill them."

"No, he didn't, but maybe if that husband hadn't seen pictures of his own wife and his business partner naked in a cheap motel room acting like he didn't exist in the world, he might not have taken a shotgun and blown the two of them away one night."

I smiled at Alex, knowing that case still stayed with him until that day. "So ignorance is bliss is what you're saying?"

"Sometimes it is."

"Are we heading out to see Mr. Sterling or is that for another day?" I asked, hoping we'd be taking a road trip that afternoon.

"I don't know if we'll be able to find him at his office on a Sunday, but if I remember correctly, he pretty much lived in that place, so it might be worth a try."

He stood to leave, closing his laptop and grabbing his notebook and pen, as I wondered aloud, "He lives in his office? Is he trying to be some gumshoe from some forties film? Does he sleep on the couch there and complain about how bad his back is from it too?"

Alex smiled at my characterization of Jefferson Sterling and shook his head. "I don't remember, but I think you might have made it way more glamorous than he really is. I think you might be disappointed if that's what you think you're going to see."

As we walked down the hallway to leave on our road trip to Sterling's office, I said, "You know, I think being a private detective might be interesting. I think I'd like that kind of thing."

Stopping right outside of Derek's office, he pushed his eyebrows up in disbelief. "It's not all it's cracked up to be. Hollywood makes it look far cooler than it actually is."

And that's when we heard Craig say, "I didn't know what to say. He as much as threatened her. I didn't know what to do. I read through the handbook, but it didn't say anything about this. I thought maybe I should tell Alex, but I didn't know what to say, Chief."

Before I could even process what Craig may have been saying, Alex walked right into Derek's office and said loudly, "I think I should be part of this conversation."

I didn't know what was going on, but I sensed it wasn't good. I walked in behind him and waited to hear some explanation.

Derek put his hands up to calm us all. "Before this gets out of control, please close the door, Poppy. This needs to stay with the four of us."

I did as he said and turned back to hear what this was all about. Craig looked downright upset, his expression dark with worry, and Alex stood with his arms folded across his chest giving off the vibe that he was ready for a fight.

What he'd be fighting about I had no idea, though.

"Alex, Craig didn't do anything wrong coming to me with this. I want you to know that he said he wanted to discuss this with you, but he didn't know how to."

In a stern voice, Alex answered, "I heard that. What I want to know is what's going on."

Craig and Derek looked at each other, and then Craig looked down at the floor as his chief explained why he'd come to him. "There's nothing to get upset about here. I just want you to know that before I tell you what's going on."

I knew Alex well enough that Derek's dragging his feet was only making this worse. Alex nodded and merely said, "Uh huh," as he waited for the chief of police to get to what had happened.

As all this was going on, I stood there with my mind racing as to what all this could be about. Who threatened who? Was this why Craig had been so strange earlier? And what did all of this have to do with me?

I sensed Alex knew a little more than I did about the situation, but at the moment, he wasn't telling anyone anything. All he was doing was standing with his arms tightly folded across his chest, letting his body language say what he refused to for the moment.

"Okay," Derek said as calmly as possible as he began once again to explain. "Craig came to see me because of a situation he didn't know how to handle exactly. I don't want anyone to get worried because I'm on top of this. It seems that Craig and Stephen were talking at the Food

King last night and Stephen had some rather unpleasant things to say about Poppy in the course of their conversation."

Alex and I looked at each other like we hoped the other person could understand just what Derek was trying to say. I turned toward him and finally blurted out, "Do they make you take special classes once you become a police chief to teach you to use all those words to say absolutely nothing?"

He grimaced from my forthrightness and shook his head. "You're not helping, Poppy."

"Well, either are you, Derek. Let's lay our cards on the table here. We overheard Craig say someone threatened some female. Was that person Stephen and was I the female?" I asked in my typical way I knew made my old friend uneasy at times.

At that moment, I didn't care.

"Well, I don't know if legally it could be called threatening," Derek said, hedging like he often did when he feared a situation was about to get out of hand.

"What could it be called then?" Alex asked in a low voice. "What did he say exactly?"

Craig lifted his head, and I thought he might break into tears he looked so upset. He cleared his throat and said in a quiet voice, "I saw him at the Food King and we got to talking. He said he heard about what happened to Samuel and that the only thing taken from his store was Poppy's ring. I swear I didn't tell him, but he knew. And then he said it would have been better if it was her instead of Samuel that got murdered."

For a moment, I felt like I couldn't breathe. I'd always known Stephen didn't like me, but I'd never actually believed that had risen to the level of hate.

However, if he was wishing me murdered, it obviously meant he truly did feel hatred toward me. I just never thought anyone would feel that way toward me since I couldn't say I hated anyone ever in my life. I didn't like Stephen at all, and after Jared broke my heart and ran away with that grocery clerk hussy, I wanted to hate him.

But I never had.

Now to know there was someone out there who actually felt hate in his heart from me made me genuinely frightened.

After I could take a full breath of air into my lungs, I looked over at Alex standing beside me and saw the rage in his expression. He'd stopped himself more than once from giving Stephen exactly what he deserved, but now that he wasn't a fellow officer anymore, I worried nothing would prevent him from finding Stephen and beating the hell out of him for this.

And then he spoke and I knew how much he was working to hold back his emotions.

"I want him taken care of, Derek. That may not meet the legal standard of a threat to Poppy's life, but it sure sounds like he has an ax to grind. She's a citizen of this town and another citizen, a police officer no less, has heard him say he wishes she was dead. What's going to be done about this?"

Derek stood from behind his desk and sighed. "I'll talk to him. He has to know this can't go any further. I don't care how he feels about Poppy. She won't be threatened by him or anyone else."

"Good. He should be glad I'm still a cop in this town or I'd give him a sample of what payback feels like," Alex said, reaching his hand down to hold mine. "But make sure you let him know he needs to stay far away from me. I'm not playing here. Cop or not, if I see him and he so much as makes the wrong face at me, I'll give him everything he's deserved for way too long, Derek."

The police chief nodded and sighed once more. Derek had never liked confrontation or fighting. That he became a cop had simply been the natural progression of his life once his brother became one. I had a feeling Derek would be far happier stocking shelves at the Food King or coaching the high school football team.

The three of us began to file out of his office, but he stopped us. "One more thing. Craig, I'm going to put you on another case, and I'm working this one with Alex and Poppy. It's not a punishment, but if Stephen does figure into this case in any way in the future, I don't want what he said to you last night to be thrown out on some technicality."

All of us stared at Derek in shock. He hadn't worked a case as an actual officer since becoming chief. Most of his days were spent cajoling the council and the mayor into letting his force have more equipment like new walkie talkies and police cruisers that didn't break down every other week. In fact, I had a sense that the wheeling and dealing he did as chief suited him just fine and far better than being a cop.

"You're working this case?" Alex asked in a stunned voice. "Is there something you haven't told us? You don't work cases anymore, Derek."

"I know I don't, but I'd never forgive myself if something happened to one of my oldest friends and the woman you're marrying in a month. Consider it to be one of my best man duties and don't make a big deal out of it. We'll just get this case solved and then I'll go back to spending my days sitting back with my feet up on my desk. That is what all you guys think I do all day, isn't it?"

"Whatever you say, Chief. As our new partner, I guess I should let you know that Poppy and I are heading to Baltimore to talk to a private detective by the name of Jefferson Sterling. It seems Samuel hired him for some work and paid him five grand."

"Okay. I'll have Craig catch me up on the case before I assign him a new one, and then I'll have a chat with Stephen."

Turning to face me, Derek smiled. "Don't worry about this, Poppy. Your groom and his best man won't let anything happen to you. I promise."

I didn't know what to say to that except thank you. It was times like this that made me happy Sunset Ridge was such a small town and everyone knew everyone's business.

Chapter Ten

ALEX DROVE SILENTLY down the highway toward Baltimore, but I wanted to talk about what had just happened. He hadn't said a word after leaving Derek's office, other than when he opened my door to get into the car and told me to watch my head as I got in.

For me, talking things out made them better. Sure, nothing much would get solved by us discussing the fact that a person he used to work with and would have put his life on the line for now openly claimed to another police officer that he wished it were me instead of Samuel killed in that jewelry store.

But that didn't matter. At least talking about it would ease my mind.

The problem was that for Alex, talking rarely made things better. Not really a person who saw much use for discussing painful ideas, he'd much rather say nothing about it, as if ignoring what Stephen said to Craig made it like it had never happened.

I'd stared out the window for nearly fifteen minutes as all these thoughts rolled around in my brain, but each passing moment made it harder to hold back from saying something about it. In truth, I needed to hear Alex say something—anything—that made me feel like I wasn't alone in this.

Which I already knew. I wasn't stupid. I knew full well that if he had heard Stephen say those horrible things about me that he likely would have cold-cocked him right there in the Food King. The thought of that actually made me smile. I imagined Stephen standing there in the canned fruits and vegetables aisle with that smug expression I hated on his face and Alex cocking his arm back far enough that when he let his fist fly, it would slam into Stephen's ignorant face like a brick into cream cheese. The image of him falling into a stack of canned peas and the cans all tumbling down on him as he fell to the floor pleased me more than it should have.

"What are you smiling about over there?" Alex asked, tearing me out of my violent fantasy.

I looked at him and smiled, happy to hear him speaking for the first time on this trip. "Cans of peas. And bricks and cream cheese."

He made a strange, confused face and then turned his head to face me for a moment before turning back to look at the road. "You mean like cream cheese icing? Are you thinking of that for the wedding cake? Because if you are, I have to say I'm not completely against that."

Chuckling, I took hold of his right hand and gave it a tiny squeeze. "No, I wasn't, but we can talk to Sherry about that tomorrow at the Charming Cakes tasting. Do you know how cute you can be sometimes?"

Alex smiled and moved into the passing lane to get around two trucks. "I have heard I can be cute. It's true. I'm not sure what I said there that was so cute, but I'm glad it made you laugh."

"I'm just glad you're talking. I was getting a little worried there for a while," I said, cautiously dancing around the subject I wanted to discuss.

He squeezed my hand gently and smiled again. "I'm about to marry a woman who is capable of talking every minute of the day. I have no illusions about not talking ever again."

"Good. Talking is something that I think can help in most situations. You know, like this one," I said sweetly, taking another step closer to the topic we needed to discuss.

I waited for his smile to fade and for him to fall silent once again, but he surprised me by simply shrugging and then saying, "I'm not sure what can be said other than you were right about Stephen all the while. He was that guy you said he was toward you."

That wasn't the direction I'd expected this conversation to take. I didn't blame Alex for wanting to believe his fellow officer wasn't actively being nasty to me. He trusted that men like himself would act professionally. I didn't blame him for that. I respected him for being so noble.

Even if I had been right all along about Stephen.

"Well, even if that is the case, that's not what I think we should be talking about."

He didn't say anything for a long moment, but when he did, it was one of those times that I knew there was nowhere else on this earth safer than right by his side.

"Poppy, I'm not going to let him or anyone else ever hurt you. If he tries anything, I'll stop him, even if that means he loses his life. I don't have anything else to say except that and I love you and part of being the man who loves you is protecting you."

When the final word left his mouth, he lifted our joined hands to his lips and softly brushed his lips over my knuckles before glancing over toward me. "I suspect you, on the other hand, have a lot more to say because that's who you are, so whatever it is you want to talk about, we have the time now."

The way he accepted who I was, even though we were so different, made me chuckle. "Well, I'm glad you aren't as enraged as you were back at the station. I mean, I like the idea of you being enraged to defend my honor and all that, but enraged Alex sort of frightens me sometimes. You get that whole Incredible Hulk vibe to you and I'm afraid you're going to tear a phone book apart or something."

He laughed out loud and looked over at me for a second. "Tear a phone book apart? When was the last time you saw a phone book anywhere, Poppy?"

Rolling my eyes, I took his teasing for what it was and said, "You know what I meant. I was channeling 1970s TV Incredible Hulk there more than the movie hulks from a few years ago."

"Whatever you were channeling, I think you're saying I have no control over my anger and I'm green. Neither of those things are good, as far as I can tell."

"Fine. You don't remind me of the Incredible Hulk. I just get worried when you get angry sometimes. You tend to bottle up your emotions so much that when you let them out, it's a little unnerving is all."

Knowing what I said was true, Alex nodded. "Well, I can honestly say that since I've been with you, Miss McGuire, I have gotten better about the bottling up emotions business. Remember, before you came along, I spent most of my time alone out at my house."

As much as I wanted to talk about Stephen and what he'd said about me, the subject of where we would live after we married had been on my mind too, along with about a million other things wedding and non-wedding related, so I took the opportunity to broach the housing topic.

"Speaking of that house of yours, what's going to happen once we get married? We won't need two houses."

He thought about my question for a long moment and shrugged. "I guess we'll sell it. I haven't been there for more than a few minutes anyway in the past six months anyway. Or maybe we can sell both our houses and find a brand new one to start our lives in."

Until that very moment he suggested selling my house in addition to his, I'd never even considered the notion that I wouldn't live in my house forever. The mere mention of it made me feel queasy, even though I didn't exactly know why.

"I'm guessing by your silence that you aren't a big fan of selling both houses?" he asked before glancing over at me.

"I don't know. I'd never even thought of it before right now."

Alex raised my hand to his lips again and softly kissed my fingers. "What if we decide to move away from Sunset Ridge at some point? We'd have to sell both houses then."

Move away from Sunset Ridge? Why was he talking about that? Who wanted to move out of town?

"Is there something you want to tell me about, Alex? Is something happening that means we'll be leaving Sunset Ridge?" I asked as my mind whirled with a dozen other questions I was too afraid to ask.

He didn't answer immediately, instead concentrating

on the road and driving past a few cars that hadn't gotten the news that the speed limit had been increased from forty miles an hour. After what felt like an eternity, he drove back into the right lane and said, "No, but you never know what the future holds, Poppy."

You never know what the future holds? What did he mean by that?

I didn't know which upset me more—Stephen spouting off in his ignorant way at the Food King that it should have been me who was murdered or the idea that at some point Alex and I would move away from Sunset Ridge. It may have sounded silly, but for all its problems, I loved the town I'd grown up in. I thought he did too.

Well, maybe not loved it but had at least come to see it as somewhere he wanted to live.

"Do you want to move away from Sunset Ridge?" I asked, unsure I wanted to hear the answer to that question.

As he took the exit and began to drive down the ramp, he casually answered, "I don't know. As long as you're there with me, I could probably live anywhere."

Anywhere? I wasn't sure what he was referring to, but I didn't think I liked it.

While I stewed over moving from Sunset Ridge and what that would mean, he drove through the streets of East Baltimore until he stopped on East Madison Street. I'd been so lost in thought that when I looked out the window at the place we'd driven to, I wondered if he'd gotten us lost.

"Did you intentionally drive here?" I asked as I stared out at dilapidated buildings and rundown houses I wasn't sure were even inhabitable.

He turned the car off and nodded. "Yeah. Jefferson

Sterling's office is just down the street."

Unsure I even wanted to get out of the car, I hesitated as he slammed his car door shut. Alex came around to my door and opened it, looking down at me with confusion as I sat there in the passenger seat not moving.

"What's wrong?"

I scanned the neighborhood and saw no one particularly dangerous looking, but the entire area just seemed so decrepit I wasn't sure I liked even being there. Something told me being in that part of the city was just asking for trouble.

"Are we going to be okay here?" I asked, still not making much progress in getting out of the car as my legs were with my head on this place being no good.

Alex extended his hand and nodded. "We'll be fine. It's broad daylight, and I have a gun. This place isn't the worst part of the city, so don't worry. You're in good hands with me."

Sure about only one thing—that Alex would always protect me—I trusted in his judgment and took his hand for help to get out of the car. Once outside, I quickly took a look around and hoped he was right. Wherever we were, I definitely didn't want to move here, even with Alex.

We walked down the block toward an old building with a red brick façade that had definitely seen better times. I imagined in earlier days, maybe even during the colonial period, it had looked stately and strong like brick buildings always seemed to look. Now, however, it looked like it may collapse at any moment.

I reached down and searched for Alex's hand as I asked, "Where are we?"

He clasped onto my hand and held it tightly, betraying how little he believed in what he'd said about this place being safe. "East Baltimore. The Old Town Mall area."

"This place is like a run-down ghost town. I hate being in places like this. It makes me think about what might happen to Sunset Ridge in the future."

Alex looked at me and frowned. "This place didn't have what Sunset Ridge has."

"What's that?" I wondered as I looked around and saw building after building that looked like no one had been in them in ages.

At least not for anything legal.

"A community that cares about what happens to the town. This area didn't have that, and once people left for the suburbs, it just kept going downhill until it ended up like you see now. Believe it or not, there was a huge shopping mall just a little ways down there a decade or two before I was born. Now it's all abandoned."

"And this is where Jefferson Sterling has his office?"

Alex stopped and pointed at the old red brick building in front of us. "Right here upstairs, if I'm remembering correctly. Ready?"

"The sooner we get done here and I get back to my cozy little town where people care what happens to it the better," I said, meaning that in more than one way.

I didn't want to be in this part of Baltimore, but I also didn't want to move from my hometown. I liked living where people cared. I knew they cared too much about the wrong things sometimes, but it still was a hundred times better than living somewhere that no one cared for at all.

The inside of the building surprised me, thank God,

and didn't feel like it would come down around our heads if a stiff wind blew or if someone slammed a door too hard. The elevator on the main floor looked usable, but after pressing the button and waiting for a few minutes, we decided to take the stairs. I took each step gingerly, afraid one wrong move could land me in the basement, but after a few didn't even creak much, I hurried up behind Alex to the second floor.

A dark hallway cut the floor in half, and two doors out of four had printing on them to say they were occupied. We passed by the first one that said Dr. Reginald Hunter, Oral Surgeon. Behind the frosted glass, people could be seen sitting down in the waiting room. I cringed at the mere thought of having my teeth worked on in this place.

Further down the hallway past two empty offices was the office of the man we'd come to see. The writing on the frosted glass in his door said Jefferson Sterling, and beneath his name in elegant script were the words Private Investigations.

Pointing at the text, I said, "Fancy. Is this an indication of what kind of person he is?"

Alex shook his head. "No. Think the exact opposite, if I recall correctly."

He rapped on the door with his knuckles, and we waited to hear someone tell us to come in. But we heard nothing from behind the door. Alex knocked again, this time a little harder, and said loudly, "Mr. Sterling? I'm Officer Alex Montero from the Sunset Ridge police department. I have some questions for you."

Seconds later, the door slowly opened and there in front of us stood a man who looked to be in his early fifties with greying brown hair who looked like he'd just woken up. Scrubbing his face, he said in a gravelly voice, "What's a small town cop want with me?"

"Jefferson Sterling, I'm Officer Alex Montero and this is my partner Poppy McGuire. We'd like to speak to you about one of your clients. Samuel Morrow," Alex said in the authoritative voice he usually only reserved for suspects.

"Samuel Morrow?" the man repeated in a surprised voice.

"Yes. Can we come in? I'd like to ask you some questions about your relationship with him."

Jefferson Sterling stepped back and opened his office door wide so we could enter. We walked into a dark room with a couch and an old portable TV to our right and a desk and chair on the back wall between two windows that had the shades drawn. He closed the door and walked past us to a small room on the left that looked to be a tiny bathroom.

"Take a seat. I'll be out in a minute. Make yourselves comfortable."

Alex and I looked around at the seating options and then looked at each other. With a chuckle, he said, "I guess it's the couch or the couch."

I leaned in close to him and whispered, "I think this guy has read one too many Mickey Spillane novels. I'd bet he wanted to put the word gumshoe on the door in that fancy lettering but someone talked him out of it. Maybe some dame he knows and sees sometimes."

As we sat down on the stiff couch, Alex smiled and said, "You know, I love your imagination."

"But?" I asked, sensing there was a second part to that statement.

He shook his head. "No but. I just love your

imagination. I would have never thought of any of that just by walking in here. To me, this is just some guy's office in a rundown building."

I placed my head on his shoulder and squeezed his arm to me. "It's a gift. And a curse. And I probably just made this guy way cooler than he actually is."

"Probably."

Just then, the bathroom door opened and Jefferson Sterling emerged looking slightly better than he had a few minutes ago. His hair, now slicked back off his face, didn't look like he'd just been sleeping on the very couch where we now sat, and his shirt was now tucked in instead of hanging out over the front of his pants. He didn't look much better otherwise, but at least he looked dressed and ready to answer Alex's questions.

"So you want to ask me about Samuel Morrow, huh?" he asked as he grabbed a metal folding chair from the corner of the room and opened it up to sit down.

"Yes. I believe he hired you right after the beginning of this year. I'd like to know what for."

Sterling hesitated for a moment and didn't reply, instead walking over to the windows behind his desk to lift the shades. As I sat there examining a room that looked even worse in full daylight, I wondered if there was some private eye-client privilege I'd never heard about. But then he pursed his lips and nodded, as if to say he understood he needed to answer Alex.

"Yeah, he hired me. Wanted me to keep an eye on someone," Sterling said as he sat down in the metal chair across from us.

"Who did he want you to watch?" Alex asked, and I sensed this meeting would be like pulling teeth trying to get answers out of this man.

But he didn't hedge his answer and immediately answered, "His wife."

I sat staring at him, surprised at how easy it had been to get that from him and surprised at the answer he'd given. So Samuel had been having his wife watched. But why?

"Did he tell you why he wanted you to keep an eye on her?" Alex asked.

Sterling nodded. "Yeah. He was worried she was cheating on him."

Excited by this news, I blurted out, "With who?"

Alex turned to look at me and gave me a tiny smile that said I hadn't broken any protocol with Sterling. We both waited for him to answer, and I silently bet that he would say the beefcake driver, Bruno.

And then he said it. "He thought she was sleeping with her driver."

God, I couldn't wait for this guy to start spilling the beans on Eliza and Bruno!

I sat practically on the edge of the couch as Alex calmly asked, "Well, what did you find out?"

As casually as if he was telling us the time, Jefferson Sterling said with a wide grin, "Well, I guess that depends on what you call cheating."

Now I was really intrigued.

Chapter Eleven

ALEX AND I leaned forward in tandem and waited as Jefferson Sterling let a pregnant pause drag out so long I wondered if he'd lost his train of thought or forgotten what he'd just said. You didn't just say something like "That depends on what you call cheating" and not follow it up with more details.

At the very least he needed to complete that thought and say if he thought she was cheating.

When he didn't say anything for nearly a full minute, Alex, who I suspected was losing his patience with Sterling's need to make everything dramatic like we were all in an old black and white detective flick, groaned and said, "Well, tell me what you saw and I'll decide if it was cheating or not, Mr. Sterling."

The man who sat across from us seemed surprised that we weren't having as much fun as he was with this interview. His smile faded, and he leaned forward toward us.

"Samuel hired me in early January, and I began to follow Mrs. Morrow around the tenth. At first, all I saw was a lady who was always driven around by a big guy. Have you met the driver yet? His name is Bruno, and he's a piece of work."

Alex wrote down the details of Sterling's story, so curious about his comment about the driver, I asked, "Why do you say that?"

The private eye smiled again and gave me a wink. "Dumb as a bag of hair, but he's got a nasty side to him, that one. Better be careful having your wife with him is what I told Samuel after the first time I watched her with that Bruno character."

Lifting his head, Alex asked the question that was on my lips. "Why? Did you see him do something violent to her?"

Sterling shook his head and scrunched up his face like the mere mention of someone being violent with a woman disgusted him. "No, not her, but I saw him get pretty nasty with a parking garage attendant that first time I followed her. He actually got out of that Beemer he drives her around in and grabbed that poor little guy working there by the collar. I thought I would have to run up and rescue him."

"Mercedes," Alex said flatly, correcting the private eye on what kind of car Eliza Morrow owned and Bruno drove her around in.

"What?" Sterling asked, now utterly confused and lost in his story.

"The car is a Mercedes, not a BMW," Alex explained in a tone of complete frustration. "A silver Mercedes."

But the correction didn't faze the man, who just waved his arm in front of him and rolled his eyes. "Mercedes. BMW. What does it matter? It's an expensive car made by foreigners."

The district attorney would have the time of his life putting this guy on the stand if it turned out that Eliza or

Bruno killed Samuel. Jefferson Sterling didn't seem to care much for specific details, except when they added to his film noir persona thing he had going on.

"Fine. So Bruno Carter got nasty with the parking attendant worker. What else did you see between him and Mrs. Morrow?"

"They act like they're either the best of friends or a couple that's been together forever. Do you know what I mean?"

I had a feeling I did, but Alex simply shook his head and said in a low voice, "No. Explain."

Sterling tilted his head back and looked up at the ceiling to take another very long pause that only served to make both Alex and me want to shake him. I knew my partner well enough to know these kinds of stage theatrics annoyed him to no end. For me, the waiting to hear another tiny snippet of information that would require more explanation just made me want to scream at the guy. We didn't have all day to be hanging out in his crappy office which doubled as a makeshift apartment that creeped me out.

"Mr. Sterling, are you having trouble remembering what you saw?" Alex said impatiently.

Still looking up at the ceiling, Sterling answered, "No, but I want to make sure I get this right." After a few more moments, he lowered his head and looked directly at us. "They do things that best friends and couples who've been together and know each other well do."

The irritation radiated off Alex. He took a deep breath and slowly let it out before saying, "Yes, I believe you mentioned that. Can you give me any specific examples of what you mean?"

For a moment, I thought Sterling might tilt his head back and return to staring up at the ceiling again. I had to hold myself back from screaming, "This isn't that difficult, for God's sake! What did you see them do?"

Thankfully, he didn't resume his examination of the dirty ceiling tiles above his head and merely nodded. "I'd see them shopping, which I think tells a lot about who this Bruno guy is to her. I mean, what man is shopping for clothes with a woman if he's just a driver? I'd also see them hanging out in the park. Do you remember that warm spell we had in late February when it was in the seventies for a few days right before the end of the month? I saw them have a picnic at Meridian Hill Park down near the fountain. They looked pretty cozy to my eyes."

For the first time in this investigation, we'd finally heard something to point to Eliza Morrow and her driver having an affair. But had he seen anything more than what may have been some innocent time at a park for lunch and what could very well be a woman dragging a man with no ability to refuse out shopping?

"Did you see them do anything that made you believe they were anything more than just two people shopping and picnicking?" Alex asked as he jotted down a note in his tablet about Eliza and Bruno's time in the park in late February, using the words FEB HEAT WAVE PICNIC MERIDIAN so he could ask them later about Sterling's claims.

All of a sudden, it seemed that the private eye had a great deal to say and didn't want to pause anymore. Maybe that whole staring up at the ceiling thing he'd done earlier was just to help him get his thoughts straight.

Jefferson Sterling stood up and walked over to his desk. As he pulled open one of the drawers, he said, "Nothing physical. No motels or hotels. No holding hands. No kissing."

He walked back over toward his seat but stopped in front of us. In his hands, he held pictures he offered Alex. "Take a look at these. I gave them to Samuel, so it's not like he hasn't already seen them. These are pics I took of his wife and the driver since January. See for yourself."

Alex took a hold of the eight by ten pictures and held them in front of us for me to see too. One by one, the pictures showed Eliza and Bruno out and about doing things that couples would do, but there wasn't a single picture of them having any physical or sexual contact whatsoever. Even the pictures of them picnicking near the fountain at Meridian Park looked complete innocent, if not strange since she was his employer and twenty years older than Bruno.

When we finished looking through every one of the more than fifty pictures he'd taken of the two of them, Alex turned and began writing notes on the images and I asked Sterling, "So never once have they gone anywhere that could be considered a place they could have a rendezvous?"

He smiled and shook his head. "I love that you used that word. Rendezvous. That's exactly what it would have been too, but no, never. They never went to any motels or hotels or even anyone's home or apartment. It was always someplace out in public like a park or a store or even a library."

His mention of a library rang a bell in my head and Alex's too, and he quickly lifted his head from his notes.

"Which library?"

This question made Sterling look toward the ceiling again, and I decided this incredibly irritating behavior wasn't intended to anger anyone. I had a feeling that was merely the way he organized his thoughts before answering.

Finally, after a few painfully long moments, he lowered his head and looked over at us once again. "The library in Caston. I saw her go there at least three times."

Alex turned toward me with a look of consternation. "She was at a library the day Samuel was murdered too."

"Yeah, Bruno said he took her to the Georgetown University Library."

I didn't have a sense that Eliza Morrow was an intellectual of any stripe, so why would she be going to the library so often? She no doubt had internet in her house and on her phone wherever she wanted to get online, so it wasn't like she needed to go to the library for that. What else did people use the library for other than books and research these days?

Sterling said, "Hey, what did you just say about Samuel?"

We looked at him, and I suddenly realized he may not have heard the news that Samuel had been murdered. Alex cleared his throat and said, "Mr. Sterling, Samuel Morrow was murdered yesterday morning. Did you know that?"

Jefferson Sterling's body sagged in his chair, and he shook his head. "No, I didn't know that. Damn, I'm sorry to hear that, though."

"You had no idea he had been murdered?" Alex

asked.

"No. I had no idea. Samuel called me last on Friday and we talked for a few minutes. He sounded fine, like he didn't have a care in the world. To hear he's dead, murdered no less, tears me up. Samuel was one of the good guys, you know? You don't meet too many of them anymore."

I nodded, once again saddened by the realization that the sweet man who ran the only jewelry store left in Sunset Ridge was gone. Alex, however, still focused on questioning Jefferson Sterling.

"I'm curious why Samuel kept having you follow his wife and her driver if you'd proven for nearly six months that she wasn't have an affair with him. We only have one payment of five thousand dollars, but knowing now what you did for that money, it seems like he overpaid tremendously. Can you explain that, Mr. Sterling?"

The private eye shifted in his seat, but unlike before when Alex asked him questions about his work following Eliza, Sterling didn't look away now. He kept his gaze focused on Alex for a minute and then shrugged.

"Following his wife and her driver wasn't all I did for Samuel. He had me do some other jobs for him, so the five grand isn't as much as you think."

Once again, I was intrigued by this man and the way he held back the details. He certainly had a way of burying the lead. What else had he done for Samuel Morrow?

Alex leaned forward and leveled his gaze on Sterling. "Other jobs? Like what?"

Sterling rubbed his hands together, which made a scratchy noise like sandpaper running over wood. "Nothing illegal. Just some checking up on people he wanted to know some more about. You can never be too sure in business, you know?"

"No, I don't know, Mr. Sterling. Why don't you make it crystal clear for me?" Alex said in a way that made the private eye understand it wasn't a request.

Sterling shrugged again and smiled. "You were close with crystal clear. He wanted me to get the dirt on a couple of his jewelry suppliers. You know, so he could have something on them he could use in negotiations for future business."

"Are you saying Samuel Morrow had you get information on people he worked with in the jewelry business so he could blackmail them to get diamonds at lower prices?" Alex asked in a voice full of disbelief.

Sterling nodded, "Yeah. Jewelry dealers of all kinds—diamonds, rubies, sapphires, whatever. He gave me their names and had me dig up any dirt on them I could. That was the main job I did for him. The job tailing his wife and that driver of hers was more of a side thing."

"Did you find a lot of dirt on these people?" I asked as Alex tried to jot down some notes but only came up with BRIBERY and a question mark.

"Some. I can give you the names and what I found on them. Nothing big. No murder or anything like that. No international crimes either. Just some petty stuff like one guy is cheating on his wife and another one has two sets of books and will probably end up in some hot water with the IRS when they find out."

"Mr. Sterling, when did you tell Samuel about what you found out?" Alex asked as he drew more question marks in his notebook.

"I met with him in late April and gave him

everything I found out on that job. He already had a lot of the pictures I'd taken of his wife and the driver, but I gave him the rest of them that day too. He didn't seem convinced, though, so he still wanted me to tail her."

"And did you see where she went to yesterday morning?" I asked, curious to know if he could corroborate the story she'd told us already.

Sterling nodded. "Yeah. The driver took her to Georgetown University and she went to the library there. She stayed there for nearly six hours and then he picked her up and took her home."

"Do you have any idea what she was doing at the library at Georgetown for that long?" I asked Sterling, wishing that Alex had pressed her more on why she'd been there.

"No idea. I sat outside the library and enjoyed the nice day while she sat inside and missed it all."

Alex closed his notebook and stuffed it into his uniform shirt pocket. "I'd like to have anything you found out about those business associates of Samuel's now, thank you."

Sterling didn't argue or give Alex a hard time about handing over the information he'd gathered for Samuel. As he searched his desk for what he wanted, I leaned over and whispered in Alex's ear, "This has been a very interesting interview, don't you think?"

He turned his head and smiled. "I'd say that's an understatement, wouldn't you?"

"I hate to think that Samuel wasn't a good guy, though, Alex," I said, hating the possibility that he was some shady businessman.

"Well, we don't have all the facts, so don't turn on him yet. All we know so far is that there's no proof that

Eliza and Bruno were having an affair, but Samuel thought they were. He also had this guy dig up dirt on people he did business with. That wasn't a crime, but it might have led to his murder. What that means is this case just got a whole lot bigger."

"I know. I'm still holding out hope he was the good guy we thought he was. What's really bothering me is Eliza's trips to the library. What's with that? What reason would a woman like her have to go to the library?"

Alex thought about my question for a moment and shook his head. "I have no idea, unless she wanted to research something only a university would have the books for."

"Like what? The phone in your pocket is a computer that help you find anything you want."

"Not everything. There are many books that haven't been digitized yet, so she wouldn't be able to find them online."

I chuckled. "Eliza Morrow isn't exactly the type of woman I think of as a scholar. Any kind of book she might want would be online or in ebook she could just buy."

My partner cocked one dark eyebrow. "So what are you saying?"

Quickly, I checked to make sure Jefferson Sterling wasn't listening in on our conversation and saw he was still searching his desk for the information on Samuel's business contacts he'd spied on. Turning back to face Alex, I whispered, "I'm saying if Eliza Morrow was using a library, she was using it as a cover for something else she was doing."

"As in?"

"Well, as in, using their computers instead of her own at the house or her phone to search for information on something she doesn't want traced back to her. I'm simply not buying that she's going to these libraries to look up rare editions of some book. She's not the type."

Jefferson Sterling clapped his hands, startling me. "Found it! I swear I need a secretary these days."

Under my breath, I said to Alex, "Yeah, a platinum blonde he calls a dame all the time."

He chuckled and quietly corrected me. "They don't call the girl who works for them a dame. She's the only female in the entire story who isn't a dame."

I nudged him with my elbow and smiled. This private eye's office was having an effect on the two of us.

Sterling walked back over and sat down in his metal folding chair again. The stack of papers in his hands made me wonder just how many people Samuel had told him to dig up dirt on.

"That's a lot of paperwork there," I said, pointing at what he held. "I guess the five grand wasn't overpaying."

He took my comment as a compliment and smiled as he said, "This is hours and hours of work here. When you're digging up dirt, it isn't like just following some lady and her driver around. This took some skill to put together. I take pride in my work."

"Well, we hope it helps us find out who murdered Samuel Morrow," Alex said before standing up and taking the stack of papers out of Sterling's hands.

"I do too. As I said, Samuel was one of the good guys." Looking at me, Sterling said, "I get the feeling you don't think so because he had me dig up some dirt on those people he works with. That's just good business, miss. You always want to know who you're sharing money with, and that's the truth of it."

Nodding, I stood up as Alex did. Maybe Jefferson Sterling was right. Maybe it was just good business to know who you were dealing with at all times. I honestly couldn't say I disagreed with that idea. I just hoped it wasn't what got Samuel killed.

"We'll be in touch if we need anything else, Mr. Sterling," Alex said as he moved toward the door. "I know where to find you."

I smiled as I passed by the private eye, and he waved at us. "I'm always here, so just stop by if you need my help. I want to see whoever did that to Samuel caught just like you. We're both on the same side."

The office door closed behind us, and we made our way past the oral surgeon's office and down the stairs to the outside where the sun shined and it didn't feel like some cheap version of a film noir movie. A woman with a tiny dog and a couple holding hands walked toward us on the sidewalk, making the area feel less abandoned than before. The neighborhood still reminded me of a ghost town, though, and I couldn't wait to get out of there and back home to Sunset Ridge.

"So that was Jefferson Sterling, private detective," I said as we walked toward the car.

Alex looked over at me and nodded. "I told you. He wasn't anywhere as glamorous as you thought he'd be. Just another guy digging up dirt on people."

As I opened my car door, I asked him, "Do you think we learned anything concrete from that whole thing with him?"

He held the driver's side door open and smiled. "I think we learned a great deal from him."

What he'd learned, other than the possibility that

Samuel wasn't as good as everyone had always believed, I had no idea. But that's why Alex was the cop and I wasn't.

Chapter Twelve

L ATE BECAUSE WE slept through the alarm and hit the snooze button two times, Alex and I raced around the house getting ready for a jam-packed Monday. Both of us had to go into work, me at *The Eagle* and him at the police station, and both of us were due at our jobs at nine sharp.

I glanced at the clock as I rushed by the nightstand on my way to the closet to grab my pink sweater and saw it was already quarter to nine. We were going to be late! Alex stood in the bathroom still dripping wet from his shower. Even worse, neither of us had made the coffee yet, and with each passing second, it became less and less likely we'd have time to.

"It's almost nine, Alex! I need to get in there to brush my teeth," I pleaded as I slid my feet into my comfortable flats.

"Okay. I'm done in here, so I just have to get dressed. We'll be fine. We live less than five minutes away from where we need to be, Poppy. Don't worry."

I pushed past him and positioned myself at the sink. The slapdash job I'd done with my makeup would have to do. Thank God I had what my mother always called a peaches and cream complexion. I rarely praised my Irish heritage, which gave me pale skin that burned after only a few minutes in the sun, but this morning, I loved that rosy glow that she'd always attributed to my being Irish.

Alex padded up behind me, still just wearing a towel around his hips, and kissed me sweetly just below my ear. "You look beautiful, like always."

Rolling my eyes, I turned my head to kiss him before grabbing my toothbrush and squeezing a thick line of blue gel onto it. "And you're going to be late, but thanks."

"You're welcome," he said, smiling at me in the mirror. "As for me being late, have you met the chief? I think he'd be okay if I rolled in a few minutes late."

"The chief is your partner on this case, so you might find Derek a little different now," I said as I brushed my teeth, garbling my words.

Alex shrugged. "I'll bring doughnuts from The Grounds. It'll placate him."

Finished with my morning work on my teeth, I rinsed the sink and turned to face him as he still stood in that towel like we had all day to lounge around. "Doesn't that seem stereotypical? A cop loving doughnuts? And will you get dressed? It's ten to!"

He slid his arms around my waist and leaned in to nuzzle my neck. "I don't think it's a good sign that my future bride is complaining about me being undressed."

My eyes rolled back in my head at the touch of his lips to my skin, and for a moment I forgot about the time, where we had to be, and everything else in the world but the two of us standing there in the bathroom. I ran my hands over the smooth skin of his shoulders, still warm from the hot shower, and let myself enjoy the feel of his strong body next to mine.

If I could stay there in our house with him like that for the rest of time, I would in a heartbeat.

But reality flooded my brain, telling me we couldn't and we had less than ten minutes before we had to be at our respective workplaces.

Cradling his face in my hands, I kissed him and reminded him of that reality. "We have to go now, so get dressed, Officer Montero."

"Fine."

He sulked away to get into his uniform while I checked my look in the mirror one last time and silently bargained with my self-esteem that I looked good enough. I was only going to meet with my boss at the newspaper. What should I care how I looked to spend a few hours with him?

"Don't forget about the cake tasting at three this afternoon. I'll probably be at the station by that time, but just in case I can't, don't forget."

Alex nodded and forced a smile. "Got it. Charming cake tasting at three. Bring an empty stomach."

As we walked down the stairs, I explained what I'd read about these wedding cake tastings. "Actually, they say don't do it on an empty stomach because it will make you nauseated. They also say to drink water between each tasting."

"Got it. Eat lunch and drink water. I feel like I'm in some kind of special training for this thing today."

I nudged him in the shoulder to let him know I didn't appreciate his teasing about this part of our wedding plans and looked longingly at the coffee maker sitting on the counter with none of my morning nectar of the gods sitting in the pot. The Grounds would have to do. I just hoped the line wouldn't be too long. I didn't need Howard in a tizzy to start off the workday.

Howard demanded I come in and report to him not only about the case, which I would have to do some of my best hedging on, but also what I'd been doing about the yearly Founders' Day celebration article that was due to him in just a week or so. As if I needed to do anything other than what I did every other year. He'd made that perfectly clear in the past, so I wasn't sure what he wanted to discuss.

At least that meant our meeting wouldn't run very long. A little of Howard went a very long way, as far as I was concerned.

ALEX DROVE TOWARD *The Eagle*'s offices, but I stopped him as he passed The Grounds. "Wait! I need to get a coffee, so just get your usual space in front of the police station. I'll walk from there."

"Oh. I figured you were late, so you'd want to head directly to work," he said as he stopped the car.

"All this time, and you still don't know me well enough to know coffee must be had before the day can begin?" I joked, leaning in to kiss him goodbye.

He smiled at me and turned the car off. "What was I thinking? And on a day you're meeting with that boss of yours? Better make it a two-cup day."

"You think you're joking, but I'm serious. It might be a two-cupper. Howard has been in rare form lately. You know he's going to pump me for information on the Samuel Morrow case. I need to be on my toes so I can do my shuck and jive dance around him so he thinks he found something out when in reality, he'll know no more than when the meeting began. Wish me luck!"

"Love you," Alex said in that sweet voice he only used with me.

"I love you too. Talk to you in a few!"

In a hurry, I ran over to The Grounds and thankfully found only two people in line ahead of me. I had a feeling the heavens were smiling down on me today. First the peaches and cream skin and now a short line for coffee, which meant I might just make it to work on time.

For a Monday, I couldn't complain. Now all I had to do was survive the meeting with Howard so I could go back to working on the Samuel Morrow murder case with Alex and then have our cake tasting that afternoon.

Not to be punny, but I thought to myself, "Piece of cake."

I walked into *The Sunset Ridge Eagle* newspaper building with a coffee cup in each hand and ready for my meeting with Howard Fleming, editor of the paper and my boss who I grew to dislike more and more each day. The man had no feelings for any of the people in Sunset Ridge, probably because he didn't even like to admit he knew people there.

But at least I had coffee. I could get through another dreadful meeting with him droning on about how the people in this town demanded truthful reporting when he continued to have me write articles that were practically complete fabrications just to appease the citizens he liked if I had coffee.

I walked toward his office at the very end of the hallway, smiling and saying hi to my co-workers as I met them going in and coming out of their own offices. Checking my phone, I saw the time change to one minute after nine just as I reached his door.

Knocking, I slowly pushed the door open as I said, "Howard, it's Poppy. I'm here for our meeting."

And then I saw it. Or rather him. My ex-boyfriend Jared. Why the hell was he here?

"Poppy, come in!" Howard said with an uncustomary excitement in his voice while he offered me a seat that would require sitting right next to Jared. "It's good to see you this morning! I think you know Jared, right?"

Know him? Yeah, I know him. All too well, as far as I'm concerned.

I pasted a smile on my face and stood frozen in the doorway. "Good morning, gentlemen. Howard, I can wait until you're done meeting with Jared. I'll just be outside in the hallway here."

"No, no. Jared's here for our meeting, Poppy, so come on in and sit down."

Jared's here for our meeting? Again the question was, why the hell was he here? This was a newspaper. Jared barely opened the paper to scan the comics, much less actual words in paragraphs. Reading had never been his thing.

I continued to force my smile, which already began to hurt my cheek muscles, and sat down in the chair next to my ex. I placed one cup of coffee on the edge of Howard's desk and clutched the other in my hand, hoping the liquid inside it would somehow give me the strength to get through a meeting with two men I really couldn't stand.

"So what's going on?" I asked, terrified at the answer that would come out of Howard's mouth.

He smiled broadly, which made his bulbous head seem even more grotesque, and looked at the man who sat next to me. "I'm happy to announce that Jared is going to be the new society page writer. Now you'll be able to spend all your time writing about crime and the police blotter."

For a moment, the words flew through the air but my brain couldn't put them together to make any coherent thought. Jared was taking my job as society writer? Not that I would miss writing all those pieces on gardens and tea parties and ice cream socials, but Jared? I wasn't even sure he could write a complete sentence.

And as much as I loved the idea of spending my time writing about crime, Sunset Ridge didn't really have much crime. At least not the kind anyone cared to hear much about. True, there had been murders in the past few years that I had worked with Alex and the police on, but other than those crimes, most of what the police did in town involved mediating neighbor disputes about parking and who should be responsible for raking up leaves from trees that shed them in other people's yards.

I stammered out, "Oh, oh...I...guess that's a good thing."

Howard nodded his head in agreement, and then came the real reason he'd called this meeting. "Well, the board decided that two part time positions would be better for everyone involved instead of one full-time position."

My surprise evaporated quickly as I saw this for what it truly was. "With a reduction in pay and benefits, I'm sure."

"It's not that bad, Poppy. I mean, you are getting married and you'll be able to be on your husband's insurance next month," Howard said still wearing that irritating smile that made his face expand so he looked like the ugliest jack o' lantern I'd ever seen.

Nice. Suddenly, I felt like I'd been transported back to sometime in the 1950s. Don't worry your pretty little head about things, Poppy. You're going to have a big, strong husband to take care of you. Oh, thank you, Howard!

All of this ran through my head in my best damsel in distress tied to the railroad tracks voice as I sat there hating my boss at that moment.

"So let's talk about how you're going to bring Jared here up to speed on the workings of the society page."

I looked over at my ex-boyfriend and wanted to laugh in his face. He had no idea what he'd gotten himself into. I knew the people who filled the articles of the society page. Jared had never bothered to take the time to even recognize they existed. Plus, the vast majority of them knew exactly what he'd done to me years ago and didn't approve.

It would have been easier for Howard to give him the crime page and police blotter. The officers on the Sunset Ridge police didn't hold a grudge for as long as the people who saw themselves as worthy of being featured on *The Sunset Ridge Eagle*'s society page. They were going to eat Jared alive.

"Well, you're going to need to get to know the players. There's the mayor and his wife, of course, and the former mayor and his wife. Don't forget that she insists on being called the First Lady, despite the fact that her husband is no longer mayor. Then there's Mrs. Scanlon, who—"

Howard held up his hand to stop me. "Whoa. He can learn all of that as he moves through the job. For right now, he's going to be working on the Founders'

Day celebration piece, so I thought it would be a great idea for you to give him the article you've written so he can jump in with both feet."

I stared across the desk at Howard in amazement. "You plan to publish my writing with his name on it?"

With not a hint of guilt, he answered, "Oh, Poppy. Don't be upset. It's not like you change the article much from year to year. I practically wrote it myself for you the first year, so in a lot of ways, it's my writing."

My heart slammed into my chest so hard I worried it might come through it like some kind of cartoon heartbeat. Unable, and more importantly, unwilling to keep my opinions on what kind of horrible boss he'd always been to myself any longer, I opened my mouth and they all came spilling out.

"You wouldn't let me write it the way it should have been, and every time I tried, you told me to basically just keep it the way it was the year before. So that's exactly what I did. But that writing is mine. Not yours, Howard, but mine. The style, the cadence of my sentences, the sound of the article is mine. I'm not just going to hand it over to anyone, least of all some guy who I'm not even sure can string a sentence together. You want him to write the society page articles, then have him write them. I'm not doing his work for him."

For a moment, Howard sat staring at me with a mixture of anger and hurt in his eyes, like I'd just slapped him across the face. He was lucky I didn't say everything I thought about him and the way he ran the newspaper. Then he'd really be smarting.

Jared dared to put his hand on my forearm and said, "We're all one big team here at the paper, Poppy. You're not acting like a team player, if you don't mind me saying so."

I jerked my head right to look at him in stunned disgust. "It's *The Eagle*, Jared. You might want to actually know the name of the newspaper you're going to be writing for. And don't you dare to say anything about me being a team player. I'm a team player all right. I know how teamwork works, pal. When you join with other people to achieve the same goal, you don't betray them in any way, shape, or form. That's teamwork, Jared. You don't know the first thing about that. You and your boss here know nothing but what you want. You, you, you. It's all about you."

For a moment, I stopped myself before saying the words that were on the tip of my tongue. I took a deep breath and then let them fly in Howard's direction.

"And you two can do all the work on this team that you want because I quit. And another thing. Those society page people are going to eat your new guy here up. They live by a set of rules you don't even know or understand. As for the crime page and blotter, consider yourself lucky if the Sunset Ridge police department gives you even the tiniest morsel of information before a case is closed and the file is locked away in some filing cabinet in Derek's office. Remember, one of them is soon going to be my husband. I'll just use my feminine wiles on him and make sure you get nothing."

Howard and Jared sat staring at me in shock. They were lucky I stopped myself from saying anything more. I stood up and grabbed my coffee cups before storming out down the hall toward my office. The rage coursing through me reached my fingers, and I nearly squeezed the Styrofoam cups to pieces. Once I closed the door to my office, I took another deep breath before I set them down on my desk and began tossing my things into a box.

My folder with all my articles went in first, and then I tossed in the pencils and pens scattered around the desk, even though they were technically the newspaper's property. I grabbed my dog-eared old copy of Strunk and White I'd picked up when I got the job there and threw it into the box. I'd been so proud of myself that day and wanted to do such a great job for the newspaper.

But I rarely got the chance to, and all the times I'd used that book to make sure my writing was the best it could be were the same times Howard had simply cut most of my words and replaced them with his own.

After I emptied the desk drawers, I saw out of the corner of my eye the little figurine Bethany had given me on my first anniversary with *The Eagle*. A porcelain grey squirrel wearing oversized glasses and sitting on a stack of books with a pencil in his hand poised to write on a scroll. She said she immediately thought of me when she saw it in a store in Frederick.

So much had changed since that day all those years ago. After her death, that horrible Samantha person took over her job and nearly all the sales staff left one by one, replaced by people more like their boss than Bethany. Now was my turn to leave.

I carefully wrapped the squirrel figurine in a couple tissues and placed it in my purse. Looking around my tiny office, I saw nothing else that belonged to me. With one last glance, I said goodbye to *The Sunset Ridge Eagle* and walked out into the sunshine of a brand new day for me.

I carried my box of things to The Grounds and sat

down at the table in the back Alex and I called ours. Every table sat empty, and even Pam seemed to have disappeared into the back, so I had the place to myself.

What would I do now that I'd quit *The Eagle*? Writing, even for a small town newspaper, had brought me more joy that I ever imagined I could find with any other career. But opportunities were few and far between in Sunset Ridge for writers.

I'd been with the newspaper for so long that I didn't know what I was if I wasn't the one who reported on society events and crime for the people of my town. Now that I wasn't that person, who was I?

More importantly, who was Poppy McGuire going to be from now on? I didn't want to be that person Howard thought I would be once Alex and I married. Some woman whose most important accomplishment had been that she found a husband. I loved Alex with all my heart, but I needed to be more than just his wife just as he needed to be more than just my husband.

As I sat there thinking about my future, I wondered if all I'd been still existed now that I wasn't that person anymore. Deep in thought, I hadn't noticed anyone approach my table and then suddenly Nate Cardow stood in front of me.

"Hi, Poppy. Are you okay? I saw you sitting in here and you looked a million miles away," he said as he smiled down at me.

"Oh, I'm fine. You know how it is," I lied. "When the effects of the caffeine start to wane, it all goes downhill from there."

"Oh sure. I get like that too. Are you waiting for Alex?"

"No. Well, sort of. I just came in here to grab a

coffee but Pam doesn't seem to be around right now, so I figured I'd just sit and relax a minute."

I made it sound like I'd just walked ten miles to get to The Grounds. Nate frowned, likely thinking I was lying to him.

"So, have the police made any progress on Samuel's case yet?" he asked, looking around at the empty coffee shop.

Knowing I couldn't share any information about an open case with anyone, I simply gave him my nicest smile and shook my head. "Not really, but don't worry. They'll find out who did it."

"I'm sure they will. Well, I guess I'll let you get back to what you were doing. See you around, Poppy."

"Thanks, Nate. See you later!" I said as he turned to leave.

Happy to be alone again, I watched as he walked out and returned to my thoughts about who I was and if the Poppy I'd always been still existed now that I'd left *The Eagle*. And then my past walked through the front door of the coffee shop, making me wish he didn't exist anymore in my world either.

Chapter Thirteen

J ARED APPROACHED ME with a smile on his face, like there would be any reason I'd want to ever speak to him again. I had to admit he was still good looking, even after the terrible things he'd done to me. But I wasn't in the market for another friend.

Even a good looking one.

Holding my hand up, I stopped him just before he reached where I sat. "Before you say anything, don't bother. I want nothing to do with you or Howard. So whatever you were planning to say, save it for someone who cares."

He stopped in midstep and frowned down at me. "I was hoping we could talk. We are still friends, Poppy. Aren't we?"

His definition of friends and mine clearly weren't the same. "We aren't friends, Jared. We've never been friends. We dated and then got engaged, and then you cheated on me with that cheap floozy from the Food King. Since then, nothing close to friends has been possible."

Pulling out the chair in front of me, he smiled. "Can I sit?"

"No! I don't want you to sit down, so just don't," I

said without a hint of equivocation in my words or my voice.

Jared either intentionally misunderstood or just completely ignored every word I'd said and sat down anyway, infuriating me. This guy broke my heart, made me question nearly everything about myself, and made me the laughingstock of Sunset Ridge. All of that made being friendly with him impossible. Why he didn't get that baffled me.

"I guess the way Howard presented that came off badly," he said, as if the last thing in a long line of insulting and irritating events surrounding him was the one that truly upset me the most.

"If that's what you've come to talk about, there's no need. I'm fine with you taking over all my responsibilities at *The Eagle*. Knock yourself out. I hope you and Howard are very happy working together. He's a joy and so are you, so I'm sure you'll get along splendidly. Two peas in a pod."

Rotten peas I'd like to feed to a pack of wild dogs.

"He didn't mean it like it came out, Poppy."

I leaned away from him and stared across the table with a mix of confusion and disgust. "Like it came out? So he didn't mean to tell me that he was taking half my job away from me and decreasing my pay by a corresponding half so you could have that job? Is that what he didn't mean to say? Because it sure sounded like that's what he meant to say."

Jared leaned forward, mistaking my body's movement as a sign to encourage him to get closer. "My mother's been bugging him for weeks to give me a job at the paper. I haven't really had a job since I got back to town, and she just wanted to help. Howard never told either one of us what he planned to do would affect you."

Now my confusion faded away, leaving only pure disgust. Was there anything more pathetic than a man in his early thirties back living with his parents and having his mother get him a job because he couldn't do it himself? Did she cook his meals for him and wash his clothes too?

Pathetic.

Pushing down the desire to insult my ex on just those points, I shook my head and once again held up my hand to stop him. "I don't care why this happened. I'm not working at the paper anymore, so have at it. You and Howard. Just make sure you go to those society ladies ready for some real insults because they're going to serve you your head on a silver platter. They don't forget anything, and if you think they won't bring up how you ran out on me for that Food King checkout girl, you're in for a nasty surprise."

My words seemed to fall on deaf ears. Jared stared across the table at me for a few moments and then sighed. "You still haven't forgiven me for what I did."

I had to stifle a laugh. So that's what he thought this was about. "Let me help you out with something, Jared. I don't need to forgive or forget what you did to live happily ever after."

Raising my left hand, I wiggled my ring finger with my engagement ring on it. "You see, I moved on. I have an incredible fiancé who loves me as much as I love him. He's gorgeous, brave, honorable, and best of all, he's a grown man. You're still a boy who's looking for forgiveness. Sorry. I can't give that to you. I'm busy giving all my good stuff to Alex."

My ex looked around the coffee shop and then turned his attention back to me. "Where is Mr. Supercop? I figured I wouldn't be sitting here two minutes before he swooped in to let me know I had to leave by giving me that squint-eyed stare he's always doing when I'm around."

"I'd guess he's working, but I sent up the bat signal when I left the newspaper, so I suspect he'll be here any moment now," I said in my most sarcastic tone.

"Always right nearby to save the day, huh?"

"Always."

Pam walked out from the back room and saw us, so she walked over to the table. "I'm sorry you were waiting. I didn't realize anyone was out here. How long have you been here?"

"Oh, just a few minutes. Not long. Can I get a large French roast, Pam?"

She smiled and nodded. "That's your third today. I don't know how you do it, Poppy, but I swear if you ever left town, I'd go out of business. Can I get you anything, Jared?"

He put a weak smile on his face and shook his head. "No, thanks. I'm good."

After she walked away, I couldn't help but say, "So you came to someone's coffee shop and you don't even buy anything? You're a real winner."

"You know I don't like coffee," he said, defending himself.

"Then buy a soda, for God's sake, but don't take up a seat in her place of business without buying something. This isn't a charity, you know."

He didn't, of course, since he likely didn't have a dollar to his name. Jared hadn't worked a full-time job since he returned to town months ago, and I suspected even his mother had grown tired of his mooching. Derek had told me in early February that he avoided spending time with his old friend because he always had to pay for him wherever they went.

"What happened to you, Poppy? You used to be so nice."

I leveled my gaze on him and stared in amazement. "Asks the person who betrayed me right before we were supposed to get married. I'm still nice, Jared. I'm nice to people I care about. I'm nice to strangers. I'm nice to little old ladies and help them across the street. The only person I'm not nice to is you."

He shook his head and grimaced. "It's a shame that you had to become this person."

Tilting my chin up, I answered his vague charge that who I'd become was something lacking or disappointing. "I'm very proud of the person I've become. I became brave after you. I became independent after you. So you can save your tsk tsking about who I've become for someone who believes your nonsense because it isn't me anymore."

Jared glanced around the coffee shop again and then turned back to look at me with a smug smile on his face. "Looks like your superhero boyfriend isn't showing. Maybe he's got cold feet. Maybe that explains why your ring was the only thing missing from Samuel Morrow's jewelry store. Maybe you're going to be left at the altar a second time, Poppy."

I heard Pam ring up my coffee on the register and stood from the table. "Maybe it's time to go home to your mommy, Jared."

Furious, I walked up to the counter and saw Pam

smiling. "It's on the house, honey."

A little of my anger faded away, and I smiled back at her. "Some guys never grow up, do they?"

"Some never do. Those we leave to their mommies. Tell Alex hi for me."

I nodded that I would and spun around to walk toward the front door without giving Jared a second look. I'd had enough of him and Howard for one day. They weren't going to get another moment of my time today or any other day, for that matter.

DEREK SAT IN his office leaning back in his chair and looking up at the ceiling. When he heard me tap on his open door, he lowered his head and smiled. "What's up, Poppy?"

"Working hard, boss?" I joked. "I guess things haven't changed much now that you're back working a case, huh?"

He sat up straight and fixed his shirt that had come out of his pants. "Not everything in police work involves running around searching for clues, you know. Just because I'm not out going here, there, and everywhere doesn't mean I'm not working."

I chuckled at his explanation, but I hadn't meant to offend him. "It's okay, Derek. I was just teasing you."

Turning to head toward Alex's office, I heard him say, "If you're looking for your fiancé, he's not in the building. He left about a half hour ago."

I peeked my head back into Derek's office and smiled. "So he's here, there, and everywhering? Did he tell you where he was going?"

"Something about this case and libraries. I'm sure

he'll be back soon."

"Okay. By the way, I just saw your buddy Jared. He's officially the new society page writer for *The Sunset Ridge Eagle*. Maybe now he can buy you pizza and beer when you guys get together."

Derek's eyes opened wide in surprise. "He got a job? Wow. But wait. Aren't you the society page writer for the paper?"

"I was until about an hour ago when Howard gave it to Jared. So I quit."

The police chief's mouth dropped open in shock. "Quit? Really? I can't believe you quit the paper. You loved that job."

He was right. I did love writing for *The Eagle*. What I didn't love so much was working for Howard.

"I did, but if he was going to give Jared the society page today, I got the feeling it wouldn't be too long before he gave him the crime page and police blotter. Now he can have all of it. Get ready because you're old friend Jared is now going to be in your life all the time just like I have been."

A sickening look came over Derek's face, and his entire body sagged at my news. "Ugh. I'm not going to like that at all. What makes anyone think he can do those two pages like you can? I think Howard's lost his mind."

"I have no idea, but he made his bed. Now he can lie in it. And when people start complaining and the newspaper starts losing money because the two most interesting columns people want to read turn into garbled messes, maybe Howard will lose his job."

Under his breath, Derek mumbled, "Jared writing anything. Sounds insane to me."

Just then, what he'd said about the Morrow murder case over at The Grounds popped into my head. "By the way, you should tell your friend not to mention things about cases that you tell him about. He was more than happy to tell me his theory of why my ring was the only one missing from Samuel Morrow's store."

Derek shook his head, squinting his eyes like he couldn't understand what I was saying. "What are you talking about? I don't tell him anything about any cases."

"I don't know, but he knew that my wedding band was the only thing taken when Samuel was murdered. If you didn't tell him, somebody did because he knows."

"Well, I didn't tell him. I need to find out who did because we can't have these kinds of leaks on any case but definitely not on a murder," Derek said, standing from his desk.

"I'll leave you to that, then. I'm going to find Alex and let him know that I'm officially unemployed."

Derek stopped next to me in the doorway. "What are you going to do now? I know you don't really need the money, but you've never not worked, Poppy. So what are you going to do?"

I hadn't thought about that at all since I said I quit and walked out of Howard's office. Now that someone had asked me what I planned to do with my life, I realized I had no real idea at all.

So jokingly, I said the first thing that popped into my head.

"Maybe I'll become a private detective. I met one the other day, and he didn't look like he had much going on. If he can do it, why couldn't I?"

For the second time, Derek's mouth fell open. "Have

you told Alex about this yet? I have a feeling he might not be too crazy about his wife being a private eye. That can get dangerous sometimes, Poppy."

I waved away his concern for my welfare and chuckled. "It's nothing set in stone, Derek. It's just something I thought of. For now, I'm just going to work with you guys on this case and get the wedding plans finalized. Other than that, I have no plans at all."

"Okay. I just want you to be careful if you do decide to become a private eye. And you're going to need to carry a gun. Don't forget that."

"Yeah, yeah. I'm more worried about seating arrangements than I am about carrying a gun. By the way, are you still a plus one? I haven't gotten a name for the guest you're bringing yet. You know I need that soon, right?"

Grinning, Derek winked. "Then I guess I better choose the lucky girl. I promise to do it by next Monday, okay?"

I tapped him on the upper arm playfully. "Looks like someone's going to have a busy week. Try not to tire yourself out there, Derek. I wouldn't want this to be too much effort."

"Don't worry. I've got it down to three possibilities." He thought about it for a second and grinned. "Well, maybe four. Five tops. But don't worry. I'll have the name of the woman I'm bringing to the wedding by early next week."

I LEFT DEREK mulling over his harem of potential wedding dates and began walking toward my father's as I called Alex. His phone immediately went to voicemail, so I left a message gently breaking my employment news to him.

"Hey, so my meeting with Howard was to tell me he was taking the society page from me and giving it to Jared. You know Jared, my ex. Well, now he's writing for *The Eagle*. So I quit. Give me a call when you can and let me know what you're up to. I mean, since I'm unemployed, I can work with you full-time on this case. Okay, call me. Love you."

Yes, I buried the lead about halfway through the message. And yes, I did start rambling there a little because I got nervous after telling him I quit my job, even though I was only telling a machine and not really Alex.

It would all work out. Derek was right. I didn't necessarily have to work. My mother had left me a lot of money when she died, and even after buying my house and my car, I still had more than enough money to live.

At least for a while. But Alex and I together had more than enough money to live on. I just hoped he didn't mind my quitting my job without at least mentioning it to him.

Not that I had planned on quitting when I walked into that meeting with Howard this morning. But just seeing Jared sitting there like he belonged anywhere near the newspaper and then hearing Howard say that he would be taking part of my job and my pay and that I would be losing my health insurance just made me snap.

Alex wouldn't care. He just told me as much yesterday. He'd probably tell me I should have let Howard have it with both barrels instead of censoring myself like I had.

Lost in my own thoughts, I didn't realize I'd walked

right down Main Street to my father's bar. I looked around the side of the building and saw the door was open. Happy that my subconscious had led me there, I walked inside and found him getting ready for a new day of customers.

"Hi Dad!" I called out as I sat down at the end of the bar just inside the door.

He turned his head and smiled. "What a surprise! I didn't expect you to come by today. What's going on that you pay your father a visit this early in the morning? Did you and Alex already solve Samuel Morrow's murder?"

"No. I think Alex is out doing some investigating on that right now. I hope we get a break soon."

"Why aren't you out with him?"

I sighed and tried to think of a way to tell my father about what I'd done. "I had a meeting with Howard at nine, so I headed there first."

My father straightened out a tray of clean glasses. "How did that go? Was he his usual charming self?"

"I quit, so I guess you can't say it went too well."

The clinking of the glasses suddenly stopped so all I heard was the whirring of the refrigerators under the bar. He looked at me with worry in his eyes but said nothing for what seemed like an eternity.

I waited for him to comment, hoping he wasn't too disappointed in me, as his words he'd always said about quitting played in my head. "Winners never quit, and quitters never win, Poppy."

"What happened?" he asked as he walked down to the end of the bar where I sat.

After taking a deep breath, I said, "He called me in to tell me he was giving Jared the society page, cutting my pay in half, and eliminating my health insurance because as he said, I'd be married soon and I could be on Alex's. What was I supposed to do, Dad?"

"I'd say you did the right thing. How dare he give that Jared a job writing for the newspaper? Can he even read?" my father asked, his tone full of acid for my ex.

"I don't think so. It's okay, though. I mean, I loved that job, but maybe it's time to move on. Alex and I are getting married, so maybe it's the perfect time for things to change."

My father twisted his face into a scowl. "That society page is never going to be the same as when you did it, honey. Just remember that. And the crime page and police blotter? Now that the paper doesn't have an in on the force, they'll be stuck with what Derek is able to tell them, which is very little. I don't think that's going to change, even for his friend."

I smiled and squeezed his hand on the bar. "Thanks, Dad. I just can't wait until the first time he has to meet with the gossips in town. Oh, are they going to give him an earful! They have never forgiven him for what he did to me, and now that Alex and I are getting married, Jared is public enemy number one to those ladies. You know how they are. They can give you a hard time, but don't let anyone else give you a hard time."

My father chuckled at my description of how things worked with the society ladies. "That's how a small town works, right? It's like one big family. You have the head of the family in those women, and if they aren't happy, then nobody's going to be happy."

I'd never thought of our town that way, but he was right. God help anyone who made those ladies unhappy. Jared was in for a real surprise with them. Good. It couldn't happen to a nicer guy.

"So what are your plans for the rest of the day now that you're free of Howard?"

"Nothing until three when Alex and I have our wedding cake tasting at Charming Bakery. Do you mind if I hang out with you until he gets back?"

A warm smile lit up my father's blue eyes. "Of course not, honey. You stay for as long as you want. My regulars will love seeing you here again. They miss you. I miss you."

I walked around the bar and hugged him. "Well, then I'll be your helper today. Now all we need are some customers."

My father poured me a birch beer and handed me the glass. "Until then, let's relax with a good drink."

At least I knew that if I couldn't find another job I could always work at McGuire's Bar.

Chapter Fourteen

A T FIVE MINUTES to three, I sat in the Charming
Cakes parking lot waiting for Alex to return any of
the four voicemails I'd left him that day or the three texts
I'd sent him in the past fifteen minutes. Cars entered the
parking lot and stopped, but none of the people who got
out were him.

Three o'clock came and I couldn't wait any longer
to go inside to meet Sherry, the wedding cake planner at
Charming. I didn't know whether to be angry with Alex
or worried. It wasn't like him to not answer my calls or
my texts.

I walked into the building and waited behind two
older ladies standing in front of the bakery display cases
choosing their pastries very carefully. One didn't like
lemon, but the other did, and they began to argue about
including one in their order instead of getting all cherry
pies for some get-together they were having two days
from then.

"A little variety is always nice," said the one with the
white hair and rosy cheeks from too much blush.

The other one, a heavy woman with grey hair,
turned to look at her like she'd just announced she hated
all pie and sneered. "Variety is fine, but lemon isn't. No

one eats lemon pies, Margery."

The first woman sulked, pouting as she said in a quiet voice, "I eat them."

Just as I was sure this would take until Wednesday for them to make up their minds, the grey haired one relented with a sweet smile for her lemon pie loving friend. "Okay. We'll get one and the other two will be cherry. Sound good?"

Margery beamed her happiness and nodded. "Thank you, Delores."

That issue settled, the women paid for their pies and went on their merry way, still the best of friends, it seemed. Delores would likely still be the bossy one, but I had a feeling Margery knew how to work around her friend's demanding nature to get what she wanted.

Sherry looked out through the bakery door window and smiled. Her chin length, wavy black hair bobbed up and down as she waved to me through the bakery door window and called out, "I'll be right there. Take a seat."

I sat down at a table and chairs farthest away from the door in an area they called the solarium. A tiny area off the bakery store, it was filled with windows that let the sun come in. Even though all the glass made it feel wide open, the warmth from the sun gave it a very cozy feel.

Looking out the windows, I scanned the parking lot for any sign of Alex. What could be keeping him? He knew the cake tasting appointment was for three. I'd reminded him that morning.

Sherry walked toward me with a tray filled with samples of cake and said loudly, "Hi, Poppy! I think you're going to love what I have for you and Alex today."

She stopped and looked around at the empty solarium around us. "Where is the groom-to-be?"

"I think he's running a little late. It's okay. We know who's going to have to make the final decision anyway," I joked, forcing a laugh.

She nodded, wholeheartedly agreeing. "It's always the bride who does. Get ready because this is the way marriage is. The woman is always having to decide."

I hated falling back on that supposed truism that men were idiots and only women knew how to do things right. That's not how Alex and I saw ourselves or wanted our marriage to be. He and I respected each other. We were a team, partners who worked on cases together and then in our private life, truly enjoyed one another's company.

The idea that at some point I would look at him like I'd seen so many women look at their husbands like they were the biggest morons walking made my stomach turn. My parents never felt that way about themselves. Never once did I see my mother look at my father like his very words and behavior disgusted her. They may not have always gotten along, but their arguments didn't change the fact that beneath everything existed a solid foundation of love that remained strong until the day she died.

I adored Alex in every way, but just as importantly, I respected and admired him for the kind of man he showed himself to be time and time again to the world. I knew he respected me too, and that respect meant everything to me. Years from now when he may be bald and wrinkled, and nature will have done its worst to me, I wanted us to still have that admiration and respect that we'd started with.

As Sherry set up her cake samples on a table behind me, I looked out the window once again to see if Alex had finally arrived. Glancing at my phone, I saw it was already ten after three. I wouldn't be able to put off starting the tasting for much longer.

"Oh, I forgot the water!" she said in a panicked voice. She rushed by me as she said, "I'll be right back with a pitcher. Just give me a second!"

She didn't have to worry. What I'd drink during the tasting was the last thing on my mind.

While she ran for the water, I quickly called him once more, but like all the other times that day, it went directly to voicemail. After listening to his deep voice tell me to leave a message, I did just that, my tone full of concern about why he hadn't arrived yet.

"Alex, it's after three and I'm at the wedding cake tasting appointment. I've called a bunch of times today, and you haven't called me back yet. I'm beginning to get worried. Are you okay? Please call me back when you get this and let me know you're okay. Love you."

Just as I clicked END, Sherry returned with a glass pitcher of water. Setting it down on the table, she smiled and said in a voice that sounded almost as worried as mine just had, "I hope you don't think I'm not prepared. I am. I just always forget the water."

Her nervousness made me want to ease her mind, so I smiled and waved away her concerns about the water. "It's fine. To be honest, I'm not sure if I hadn't read up on these tastings that I would have thought of having a glass of water, but I guess with all the tastes and all the sweetness, water's a good idea."

My words made her relax, and she sat down at the table with me. "Thank you for saying that, Poppy. I sometimes get a little flustered with things. Now, are you ready for some cake tasting? I have what you and Alex asked for, in addition to a few that are a little wilder and a few of the more traditional choices. Feel free to ask me anything you want. I'm here to make sure that you get the cake you absolutely want for your big day."

I took one last look out the windows to see if Alex had arrived and my heart sank. I'd have to do this cake tasting without him.

"Okay, let's do this," I forced myself to say.

The last thing I wanted to do at that moment was eat sample of eight different cakes.

"Great! We always start off with the lighter and fluffier cakes first. The fillings and frostings are separate, so once you find a cake you like, we'll move onto those. You're definitely going to need the water then."

Sherry jumped up from her seat to bring over the tiniest and cutest piece of white cake I'd ever seen. I looked at the table behind me and saw all the pieces were the same size. They looked like someone had baked eight little doll-sized cakes and cut a wedge from each. Obviously made for just a few bites, probably enough for the groom and bride to try each variety, they were the cutest little things.

Placing it in front of me, she explained, "This is angel food cake. It's definitely light and fluffy, and for a warm weather wedding, it's quite popular. Give it a try and see if you like it."

I picked up the fork sitting on the plate and sunk it into the first cake sample to cut off a bite. As soon as I tasted it, I had to admit it was delicious. Sweet yet not sickeningly so, it practically melted on my tongue.

"Oh, I like that. I've never had wedding cake that

tasted like this. Most of the ones I've tasted are heavy."

Sherry shook her head, making her curls swing left and right. "Oh, I know. And then they put on that frosting that makes you feel like you're going to be sick. But this is so light. I love it for wedding cakes!"

Her enthusiasm began to push away my unhappiness that Alex had stood me up for our one and only cake tasting appointment, so I took another tiny piece of the angel food cake and had to admit it might not be necessary to try any others I loved it so much.

Pointing at it with the fork, I nodded. "This is definitely going to be in the running, no matter how great the other ones taste. I just love how light it is."

Thrilled I'd found one I liked already, Sherry beamed. "Okay. Great! I'm going to put this over to the side in the area I'll call definitely a possibility."

She poured me a glass of water and stood up from her chair again. "Let me get another one, but take a drink of water to cleanse your palate."

The next cake she placed in front of me instantly made me think of the beach. I didn't even have to taste it to know it contained coconut as the scent wafted up to my nose. Another white cake, this one looked a little less fluffy and a tiny bit denser.

"This is a coconut cake, and it's usually paired with a lime frosting, but that's entirely up to you. Take a taste of the cake and see if you like it," Sherry said as she poured more water into my glass.

This one tasted creamy and rich and reminded me of a piña colada. It wasn't bad, but I didn't think it would be right for our wedding.

I pushed the plate away after just one bite. "I don't think that will work. Neither of us are huge coconut fans."

For a moment, Sherry looked disappointed, but her buoyant attitude toward this whole cake tasting thing rebounded almost immediately. Shunning the coconut cake to the other table, she returned with a third variety that looked nothing like the first two as I washed away the remnants of the coconut flavor from my mouth.

A slice of red velvet cake sat in the middle of the plate in front of me looking decadent and heavier than the previous two choices. I knew almost instantly that I didn't want a red colored cake for my wedding, but I humored Sherry, who looked like she wanted to explode she was so excited about this cake.

"It's a little wilder, but it tastes divine!" she squealed as I took my first bite.

I had to admit it did taste good. I couldn't place exactly what it tasted like since it wasn't chocolate or vanilla or even like the angel food cake.

"It's very good, but I don't think I'm a red velvet kind of bride," I said with a smile, pushing the plate toward her to place it in the banished section with piece of coconut cake.

Sherry carried away the unwanted cake to the other table, and I took another drink of water, wondering how people drank so much water and ate so much all in one setting like this. At this rate, I'd be floating away or bouncing down the road after so much water and cake.

As I considered telling her that I'd already made up my mind and wanted the angel food cake so we could move on to the frosting that would work with the flowers I wanted, I saw Bruno Carter come through the front door of the bakery and walk up to the counter. As handsome as the last time I saw him, now he wore a grey dress shirt with black dress pants instead of jeans and a t-shirt, but his nicer clothes hid nothing of his very muscular body.

After she put down another plate in front of me, Sherry looked behind her to see who I was watching and whispered, "That's Eliza Morrow's driver. He doesn't look like any driver I've ever seen. He's not exactly Morgan Freeman in *Driving Miss Daisy*, is he?"

No, he wasn't.

I didn't respond to Sherry's question, which encouraged her to keep talking. "I heard some people say at Diamanti's last night that they thought he might have killed poor Mr. Morrow. I guess since he's walking around looking like that and not wearing a prison jumpsuit that the police haven't been able to arrest him yet."

Although I knew I shouldn't say anything about the case, I didn't want Sherry to think that anyone guilty would be allowed to walk around free by the Sunset Ridge police, so I whispered, "I don't think he's a suspect so much as a person who might know something. But don't worry. The police will find out who did that to Samuel and put them away for a long time."

Bruno Carter finished buying whatever he'd come to Charming Cakes for and walked out without looking over at Sherry and me. Once he'd left, she turned back toward the table and said, "What do you think a man who looks like that is doing driving around Eliza Morrow?"

I honestly had no good answer for that, but I had my suspicions.

"Have you ever spoken to him?" I asked Sherry while she looked out the window as he drove away in

Eliza's silver Mercedes alone.

When he was out of sight, Sherry looked at me and shook her head. "No. I just see him around every so often. Sometimes he comes into Diamanti's for a drink late at night just before the restaurant closes. He never seems to speak to anyone."

As I filed that information away to tell Alex later, I said, "Well, he's not the sharpest tool in the shed, if you know what I mean. Maybe that's why he's working as a driver."

Nodding, Sherry smiled knowingly. "Big and dumb, huh? Isn't that always how it is? The gorgeous ones are dumb, and the brainy ones who can make good money look like something only their mama can love. But you got a man who's both good looking and smart with a great job. Alex is definitely a keeper."

I smiled even as I wondered why my keeper had stood me up for our cake tasting date. "Yes, he is. I think I want to go with the angel food cake, so let's move on to the frosting that will work with the flowers I want on top of the cake."

THE CAKE TASTING behind me, I drove past the police station and didn't see Alex's car parked out front, so I headed home. He wasn't at the house when I got there either, though.

Something felt wrong. Alex never just disappeared for an entire day like this.

I began to worry that he may have been hurt, so I called Derek to see if he'd heard anything. He hadn't and didn't seem particularly concerned. That didn't mean anything, though. The world could be blowing up around him and Sunset Ridge's police chief wouldn't be worried.

But I was.

I brewed a pot of coffee to add to my nervousness and called my father. He hadn't seen Alex at the bar in days and certainly not in the two hours since I left.

Ending the call, I tossed my phone on the kitchen table and began to pace back and forth through the house from the front door to the back door. Had Alex found a clue in the Samuel Morrow case that he left to follow? That would definitely be something he'd do, but if so, why had his phone kept going directly to voicemail?

As the minutes turned into one hour and then two, my mind began to play its usual tricks on me. On one pass through the house, I finished my second cup of coffee and wondered if Jared had been right.

Maybe Alex had gotten cold feet.

Maybe that's why he didn't show up to the wedding cake tasting appointment.

Maybe he didn't want to get married.

Or more correctly put, maybe he didn't want to marry me.

I needed to talk to someone before my doubts took over. Grabbing my phone, I called Holly and prayed to God she had a few minutes in between patients to chat so I didn't let my worry run away with me.

"Hey, Poppy! What's up? Oh, I meant to call you today. The bridesmaid dress will be ready this Friday, so I'm going to drive down and do one last fitting on Saturday. I don't think you need to be there, but if you want to grab lunch, I'd love it."

Continuing to pace toward the front door, I said,

"Yeah, that sounds great."

"Is something wrong? You don't sound okay."

I stopped at the front door and peered out the tiny windows at the top to see outside. Still no Alex.

"Yes. I mean I don't know. Alex didn't show up for the cake tasting appointment at Charming Cakes this afternoon. I've been calling him all day and it keeps going to voicemail, and he hasn't answered not one of my texts."

I took a breath and then said the words that had settled into my mind. "I think something's wrong."

Holly remained silent for a moment and then asked, "Do you think he's been hurt? It is Sunset Ridge, and while you have some crime, I doubt anything's happened to him."

"That's not what I'm worried about. Alex can handle himself on the job. I'm worried it's something else," I said, hating how self-doubt had already begun to overwhelm me.

Why did Jared have to show up in my life today and say those things?

But Holly wasn't believing any of it. "Something else? Like what? Like you think he missed the cake tasting on purpose because he doesn't want to get married? That's it, isn't it? You're thinking he's going to do what Jared did."

Quietly, I admitted that's exactly what had worried me for hours. "Maybe he got cold feet, Holly."

"I don't believe that for a second. Alex isn't Jared, so whatever you're thinking, don't. The man is crazy in love with you. Don't worry. He's probably out doing something for work. That's all. I'm telling you, Poppy, don't worry."

As much as I wished I didn't believe that, my mind raced with possibilities, and they all involved Alex deciding he didn't want to get married, just like Jared had a few weeks before the wedding.

What if the past was repeating itself?

Knowing Holly wouldn't hear of Alex doing anything like that, I lied and pretended like our conversation had helped me. "Okay. You're probably right, Holly. I'm sure you are. Thanks."

"Okay, honey. Lunch on Saturday when I come down to Michelle's?"

"Sounds good. Text me what time you're coming."

I ended the conversation and checked my messages for a text from Alex. Still nothing.

Walking into the kitchen, I looked up and saw the clock said it was almost five o'clock. According to what Derek told me, he'd been gone since before ten that morning. Where had he gone and why?

And was it to track down a lead on the Morrow murder case or for some other reason I couldn't bear to even think about?

Where could he be that he hadn't gotten any of my voicemail messages or texts?

Chapter Fifteen

AFTER ANOTHER THIRTY minutes of pacing, I heard a noise outside and looked to see his car in the driveway. I watched Alex walk up the front steps and onto the porch, not seeing any outwardly visible reasons why he wouldn't have gotten my calls or texts. He didn't look injured or like he'd just spent the day at the hospital, thankfully.

That reason eliminated, I still wondered what had happened to him.

He opened the door and walked in, surprised to see me standing there in the middle of the living room. Closing the door, he smiled like nothing was wrong.

That alone made my emotions turn from worried to angry. If nothing was wrong, why did he miss the cake tasting?

"Poppy, I didn't expect to see you standing right there when I came in."

"No? Where should I be then?" I asked, my anger at him being perfectly fine and still missing the appointment rising by the second.

I knew it made no sense, but there it was. If he had been hurt, I would have been devastated, but at least I would have known why he stood me up at Charming's.

Since he was perfectly fine, all I had left was anger that he'd left me waiting for him there with no text or call to say why.

He walked up to me and cradled my face in his palms before kissing me softly on the lips. "I'm sorry I missed the cake tasting thing today. Did you still go? I know whatever you picked out will be fine."

Leaning back, I stared up at him in amazement. Did he think that's all it would take to make this okay? An apology and telling me whatever I chose would be fine?

"Why didn't you show up, Alex? We waited for you. It was embarrassing to have to do that without the groom-to-be."

He pulled me into a kiss and said quietly, "I know. I'm sorry. I wanted to be there. I did. I just got stuck in traffic."

My mouth dropped open in shock at his lame excuse. "You got stuck in traffic? That's why you couldn't text me or return one of my calls all day? I called you like five times today, Alex. You were stuck in traffic all day and couldn't use your phone? That sounds like one hell of a day. Too bad mine was worse."

Alex let me step away from him and shook his head, clearly confused about why I seemed so unhappy. That he didn't understand only made things worse.

"I know I was supposed to be there at three, Poppy, but it's not like I missed the actual wedding. As for my phone, it's been dead since this morning. I forgot to charge it last night, so I've been without one all day."

His casual way of saying that he didn't care about the cake tasting made me want to scream. "That meant something to me today, Alex. I get that you don't care what kind of cake we have at our wedding, but I do. Just like I care about the bridesmaid's dress and the invitations and everything else I've taken care of for our big day, which is starting to feel like my big day and your whatever day."

Just like every other time in my life when I became that angry, tears filled my eyes, threatening to spill out and make me feel stupid. I hated that when I got mad this happened. It made people think I was sad when I was actually enraged.

Especially men, who never understood that my tears were a sign that I wanted to yell and throw things more than be held like some pathetic creature who didn't have control of her emotions.

I turned away and began walking toward the kitchen to give me a chance to dry my eyes, hopefully before he saw any evidence that I'd started to cry. I didn't want to be hugged. I wanted answers.

He came up behind me and did exactly what I didn't want him to do. He tried to put his arms around me, but I turned out of his hold and shook my head.

"Don't treat me like I'm some breakable thing you need to coddle. Just tell me why you couldn't make it to the one thing I needed you to do with me today?" I asked, refusing to look at him while my emotions still ran rampant inside me.

Alex didn't speak for a few moments and then quietly said, "I drove to Georgetown to see why Eliza Morrow was at the library the day Samuel was murdered. It took me a long time to get the person who was working that day so I could ask him some questions. On my way back, I got stuck in a traffic jam and sat there for three hours while some ten car pile-up was cleared from the highway."

I listened to every word he said, each one measured and calm like always. Typical Alex. I believed every word too. I had no reason to think he'd lie about what he'd been doing. My self-doubt was in full blown mode, but I wasn't insane.

When he finished, I wiped under my eyes and turned around to face him. He stood there looking at me like he worried I might break into a million pieces, but he said nothing. So as calmly as he'd told me about his day, I reported to him about mine.

"Our wedding cake is going to be angel food cake. I liked how light it tasted, so it's perfect for a late spring wedding. Sherry told me the kind of icing that will work with the flowers I want, but at the moment I can't remember the name. There won't be any filling. And I quit my job at the newspaper because Howard hired my ex to write the society page, which meant that my pay would be cut in half and I'd lose my health insurance. So I quit."

Alex's eyes opened wide as my words sunk in, and then they returned to normal. The expression on his face changed from worry to surprise to what I thought looked like confusion. I didn't stand around waiting for him to say anything, though, and walked upstairs to the bedroom to lie down.

This day had been too much. I needed a nap.

I CURLED UP under the covers and pulled them over my head, hoping to shut out everything so I could quiet my brain and find some peace. For hours, that tiny voice that had terrorized me so many times since that day I found out Jared had run off with another woman had been screaming in my head that the past was about to repeat itself.

That Alex would get cold feet and run away just like Jared did.

It didn't matter how many times I told myself that would never happen. That Alex wasn't Jared and I had no valid reason to believe he didn't want to marry me as much as I wanted to marry him. Nope, it didn't matter. The voice kept repeating its ominous warning over and over until that's all I could focus on.

Alex is going to leave you just like Jared did. Alex is going to leave you just like Jared did. Alex is going to leave you just like Jared did.

And there's nothing you can do to stop it because it's you he doesn't want.

My head pounded from the sound of those words echoing in my brain. My stomach had tied itself into a tightly wound knot just as Jared sat down at the table at The Grounds all those hours ago, so by the time I curled myself up into the fetal position and pulled the covers up over my head, the pain in my gut hurt so bad I wanted to cry.

I hated that I was so weak that a few well-chosen nasty words from my ex could send me spiraling into this kind of paranoia and self-doubt that practically crippled me. I felt foolish even admitting to myself that he still had that effect on my psyche.

As all these thoughts swirled around in my head in a toxic soup that threatened to poison every inch of me, I heard Alex come into the bedroom. A sense of embarrassment washed over me as I listened to him untie his shoes and toss them across the room and then felt the bed dip when he sat down.

He must think I'm crazy. I wouldn't blame him if he didn't want to marry me because I'm nuts.

Without saying a word, he crawled under the covers with me and gently put his arm around my body, pulling me to him so we were pressed together. He rested his chin against my shoulder, and his warm breath drifted over my cheek.

But he said nothing.

For Alex, words were necessary evils like other things in life that one was forced to have. He preferred to show people what he believed and how he felt about them rather than tell them. While I loved words and had an overabundance of them inside me just waiting to get out most days, he could easily not speak a single syllable on any given day and he would have been happy.

Sometimes that frustrated me. Now I loved that he didn't fill the air with words he hoped would help or wasn't sure were even what he should say but felt the need to because he didn't like seeing me like this.

His silence soothed me, and the strength I felt from having him there next to me made that voice that had been screaming for hours slowly fade into the recesses of my mind. I sighed, letting the stress of the day out.

"I'm sorry."

He likely had no idea what I was apologizing for. That's okay. It was more of a blanket apology anyway.

"I didn't mean to scare you today, Poppy. I wasn't in any danger, though. It was just some basic investigating," he said quietly in my ear.

"That's not why I was upset," I said as I pulled his arm tighter around me so I could feel him even more.

"You were too good for that job anyway. Don't worry about that. They'll be calling you begging you to come back before Founders' Day. You watch," he said, trying to be sweet.

I brought his hand to my lips and kissed his knuckles before tucking it under my chin and snuggling around it. "I wasn't really upset about that either."

Alex said nothing in response, but I wanted him to know why I'd been so upset all day. I rolled over to face him and closed my eyes. I couldn't stand to see the look in his dark brown eyes when I admitted the truth of what happened to me since kissing him goodbye that morning.

"After Howard gave Jared the society page and I quit my job, I was sitting in The Grounds trying to get my head around what I'd just done. Jared came in and wanted to talk, but I told him to go away. He…he said you were probably getting cold feet like he did about marrying me."

I buried my head in the pillow. "I know it was stupid to let him get to me like that but then—"

Alex pulled me into his arms and held me to him before finishing my sentence. "But then I didn't show for the cake tasting and you thought maybe he was right. I'm sorry, Poppy. I never meant to make you think that. It was just a cruel coincidence that I got stuck in traffic and didn't make it. You know that, right?"

I turned to face him and saw the worry in his eyes. I'd never seen that in any other man's eyes when they looked at me.

"I know, Alex. This actually has very little to do with you. It's all in my head. I let him get to me, and I don't know why. I have a wonderful man who never makes me doubt for a second that he loves me, but all that tiny voice in my head needs is one shove from my ex and I end up spending the day going out of my mind thinking that you're going to do what he did. It's crazy. You're marrying a crazy woman."

He smiled and shook his head. "You're not crazy, but even if you are, I don't care. I still love you, Poppy McGuire. And I'm not going anywhere. You're stuck with me."

Then he kissed me softly, and the last faint sounds of that awful voice in my head faded into nothingness.

Slowly, as I lay there in Alex's arms, my stomach began to untie itself from that wretched knot it had been in for hours and my headache subsided. We said nothing more for a long while as I relished the quiet strength of my soon-to-be husband who could never know how much this woman who loved to talk appreciated what he gave me.

I kissed him on the cheek once I felt better and asked, "So what did you find out today?"

Leaning back, Alex smiled. "Some very interesting things that make me even more interested in Bruno Carter for this murder."

My curiosity piqued, I urged him to tell me more as I propped my head up on my hand. "Really? What did you find out?"

"He's definitely not what we thought he was. He's not sleeping with Eliza. That's for sure."

"Why? How do you know that? Did you find some secret wife or something today?" I asked, intrigued about what Bruno Carter's story was.

Alex shook his head. "No secret wife, but I found out about a secret baby. Seems Eliza is Bruno's mother. She gave birth to him when she was fifteen, and her mother passed him off as her own so Eliza wouldn't have to drop out of school."

"Ooooh. I doubt most people would think Eliza Morrow would be associated with something so sordid. Who's the father?" I asked, intrigued about Samuel's wife even more now.

"This is where it gets sordid. The father was some college kid at Georgetown who she was dating. She was fifteen, and he was twenty-one and about to graduate. He heard about the baby and wanted nothing to do with it. So her mother raised the child."

The story about Eliza being at the Georgetown University library the day Samuel was murdered now seemed to make sense. "Is that why she was at the library on campus on Saturday?"

"I think so, but I'm not sure specifically why yet. And it doesn't explain what she was doing at the Caston library those other times. But I have a theory."

"Tell me! This is getting good," I squealed, happy to be back on the case and out of my own head after a long, trying day.

"I've got a better idea. Why don't we take a ride over to the Caston library now and see what we can find out? You up for it?"

I threw off the covers and jumped over him to the floor. "More than up for it. Let's go!"

"I need to get my shoes on, Poppy. So do you," he said as he rolled out of bed.

"Get your shoes on and give me a couple minutes to fix my hair since I have bed head. Then we can get going," I called back to him as I hurried into the bathroom.

I brushed my hair and then headed back into the bedroom just as Alex finished putting his shoes on. "I had a feeling Bruno wasn't just a driver, but I have to admit I didn't peg him for a relative of hers. That's a surprise."

"Take a look at their eyes the next time you see them together. Something told me the similarities weren't a coincidence, so I headed down to D.C. to see if it was possible that's why they are so close," Alex said with a grin.

As I straightened out his uniform shirt, brushing out the wrinkles with my hand, I couldn't help be impressed with him. I'd been right there when we spoke to Eliza and Bruno, yet I hadn't noticed their eyes looked alike.

"I didn't see that at all," I admitted sheepishly.

Alex kissed me sweetly on the lips and smiled. "You were too busy checking out Bruno's muscles. Ready to go?"

WE DROVE UP to the Caston Public Library on Broad Street, and Alex parked the car right in front of the old Federalist style brick building. As the two of us walked up the stairs to the front door, I looked for the usual plaque that these kinds of places had right next to the entrance bragging about some famous historical person having done something important on that very spot.

Alex saw me searching for it and joked, "I think this is the first old building I've seen since I moved out to Sunset Ridge that doesn't have a plaque saying George Washington slept here or something equally historically dubious."

"Maybe he wasn't in the mood for books when he was in town. He was a very busy man, you know. That war wasn't going to win itself," I said as Alex held open the glass front door so I could walk in first.

I stopped just inside the entrance as the scent of books hit my nose. I loved the smell of books. Old books, new books—it didn't matter. They all smelled so warm and wonderful. They reminded me of when I was a little girl and my mother would take me to the library every Saturday to pick out that week's books.

My partner ran into me from behind as I reveled in the scent of the library around me, sending the two of us careening forward toward a table of children's books. Thankfully, we caught ourselves before the entire bunch of them landed on the floor along with the two of us.

"You have to tell me when you're stopping, Poppy," Alex said as he straightened himself.

"Sorry, I got lost in the smell of all these books for a second."

He looked at me strangely for a moment but didn't ask me what I meant before turning toward a desk where a woman sat in the back corner of the room. I took one more deep inhale of the wonderful smell of the library and followed him over to her.

A young woman I guessed to be in her late twenties or early thirties, she had dark blonde hair that hung just below her shoulders and sat writing in a notebook. As we got closer, I saw her ears were pierced no less than six times each all the way up to the top of the outside of her ear. Each earring was a hoop, and it made her ear look like the waist of a pair of pants that needed a belt.

She lifted her head from her work as we approached the desk, and I saw her nose was pierced and contained the same kind of small hoop earring her ears had. The woman smiled up at Alex and me, but all I could think about was how much all that piercing must have hurt and then immediately my brain traveled to how much all those hoop earring must cost to fill all those holes.

Alex seemed to read my mind because he turned and the expression on his face said, "Don't mention the piercings."

"Excuse me, miss. I'm Officer Alex Montero of the Sunset Ridge police and this is my partner, Poppy McGuire. We're looking for some information about someone who's come into the library a number of times in recent months."

He pulled Eliza Morrow's picture out of his shirt pocket and asked, "Have you seen this woman here at any time recently?"

The librarian took the photograph from Alex and studied it for a moment. A look of recognition came over her, and she nodded before handing it back to him.

"Yeah, I have seen her here once or twice."

"Her name is Eliza Morrow. Would you be able to tell me what she was looking for here?" he asked, but I doubted even the best librarian would remember a detail like that.

She shook her head no, but immediately turned in her chair and began typing on the old desktop computer on the corner of the desk. "Eliza with a z, right?"

"Yes. Eliza Morrow," Alex said as she tapped away on the keys.

A list came up on the screen in front of her, and she ran her fingertip from the top down, leaving a trail in the dust on the computer monitor. "She's checked out a number of books. Moby Dick, The Rise and Fall of the Third Reich, Hollywood Wives, and The Beginner's Guide to Making Wreaths."

Alex wrote the titles in his notebook and then

glanced over at me. If I'd ever heard of a more eclectic reading list, I wasn't sure where.

"That's a strange grouping of topics," I said with a chuckle to the librarian. "Classic literature, Nazi history, romance, and a do-it-yourself book on wreath making?"

She nodded and smiled. "I'd say so. But here's something even stranger. Each time she took the book out for only a day and then returned it. Unless she's done that speed reading course they used to advertise for, I'd guess she isn't reading them. At least not Moby Dick and the Nazi book."

Alex looked around the tiny library and asked, "Are those books checked in now?"

The librarian looked at the screen again and nodded. "Every one of them. The two fiction books are in the stacks on the left side of the room arranged by the author's last name. In this case M for Melville and C for Collins. The other two nonfiction books are on the right side of the room, the wreath book in the seven hundreds and the Third Reich book in the nine hundreds in history."

He thanked her for her help and pointed toward the nonfiction side of the library. "You take that side and I'll find the fiction books. We'll meet up at the tables in the middle of the room when we find them."

"What am I looking for when I find them?" I asked, more than a little confused about what we were doing.

"I don't know, but that selection of books is odd, to say the least, and keeping each book for just one day tells me she wasn't checking them out to read them."

He headed off to find the two fiction books, so I walked across the room to the nonfiction stacks and searched for my two. It took less than a minute to find my assigned books, and by the time I sat down at the tables, Alex was coming toward me with his two.

"Okay, we have them. What do we do now?"

"Open them up and thumb through them. See if there's anything like a note or any pieces of paper left in them."

I did as he said and began looking through the wreath-making book. Each page gave very detailed instructions on how to create handmade wreaths, but there were no papers whatsoever between the pages.

"Wreath book is clean. Just a whole lot about wreaths. Now onto the Third Reich."

Sliding the book toward me, I marveled at its size, especially for a one night read. "There's no way she read this book in one night." Flipping to the end, I said, "It's over a thousand pages!"

Alex looked up as he finished leafing through Moby Dick and nodded. "That's why I wanted to see the books. Keep checking."

I flipped through each page of the rise and then the fall of Nazi Germany without finding anything. Meanwhile, Alex finished his inspection of Jackie Collins' Hollywood Wives and pushed the book away in disgust that his hunch had been wrong.

"So much for going old school," he mumbled.

Just before I reached the end of the massive tome in front of me, I felt something behind the page I was turning. I looked down and there in the last few pages was a piece of paper.

Excited, I held it up for Alex to see. "Hey, look at this! You might have been right."

His face lit up, and he leaned forward to check out the piece of paper. "Does it say anything?"

It was a piece of notebook paper folded in half and ragged on the sides. I opened it up and saw someone had written on the top two lines in large letters, "FRIDAY NIGHT 10PM BEHIND THE BUILDING."

I handed Alex the paper, and he read it too before looking across the table at me with dejection in his eyes. "Not too helpful. This could have been any Friday at ten in all the years this library has been open and who knows what building this person was referring to."

"Wait a second. Don't get down on this just yet. We can figure out a few things at least. It's definitely a man's handwriting. It's all flinty looking, so definitely a man's."

Never a huge fan of my handwriting ideas, Alex raised his eyebrows in disbelief. "Flinty? You want to explain what you mean by that?"

I held up the paper and pointed at the sharply written letters. "Females have a rounded nature to their writing nine times out of ten. It's just how it is. I don't know why. But men tend to have a straighter feel to their writing. Also, women usually don't print. Not even younger women. Printing is a guy thing, and this printing is very angular. That's why I said it's flinty."

My explanation didn't impress him, and he took the sheet of paper back as he mumbled under his breath, "Flinty printing."

The librarian walked over to the table and pointed at the books. "Oh, good. I didn't know if you'd find them. Hey, that's probably Gavin's. It looks like his writing."

I thought Alex's eyes were going to come right out of their sockets. He spun around in his chair to look up at her and said excitedly, "Gavin who? How do you know this handwriting?"

"I can't be absolutely sure, but it looks like Gavin O'Malley's writing. He's one of the fill-in daytime librarians here. He comes in when someone calls in sick."

Instead of asking her anything more about this Gavin person, Alex quickly took out his notebook and began flipping through the pages. Wanting to know more, even if my partner didn't, I asked her, "Do you know where we can find him? Does he live in Caston?"

She shook her head, which made the hoops in her ears move too. "No. I think he lives in Baltimore or D.C. He's not a volunteer, though, like the rest of us. He's some bigwig with the library system, I think."

The librarian walked away to tend to another group of people who had walked in just before I asked her about Gavin, and Alex held up his notebook to show me what he'd written on one of the pages.

GAVIN O'MALLEY, BRUNO'S FATHER

Chapter Sixteen

B RIGHT AND EARLY at seven on Tuesday morning, Alex and I stood outside on the front porch of Gavin O'Malley's upscale home in Columbia, about an hour southeast from Sunset Ridge. Unlike the wrap-around porches on the Victorian homes in our town or even my modest porch that spanned the entire front of my very average size house, O'Malley's home had merely a small covered area right in front of the door, despite the fact that his home was at least twice the size of mine.

Painted light grey with black shutters, the stately Colonial stood proudly on a sizable lot that also included a circular driveway, a yard big enough for children to play in, and a two car garage. Around the neighborhood, tall trees towered over the homes creating a canopy of leaves that let in just the right amount of sunshine. I had to admit I liked this place.

When no one answered after the first knock, I nudged Alex's arm and said, "This is a nice neighborhood. Don't you think? Very safe feeling."

He smiled and knocked again on the front door. "Except for the possibility that the man who lives here killed a jeweler in cold blood. Other than that, yeah, it's pretty nice."

I rolled my eyes at his insistence on always being a cop. "You couldn't just comment on the trees or how cool it is that there are no mailboxes in front of any of the houses? I like that idea of having to go down the road to collect the mail. I bet it gives everyone a chance to get to know one another."

"I bet it's a pain when it's winter and the last thing you want to do is walk all the way down the road to get your mail," he said, countering my approval for the way the area had been set up.

That he had a point didn't change my mind about how lovely and bucolic the neighborhood was, faraway mailboxes and all.

Changing the subject back to the reason we stood there on that porch, I looked up at the bedroom windows on the second floor and saw no one moving around. "I don't think anyone's home, Alex. Maybe they've all left for the day?"

His eyebrows shot up in that way they did when he doubted what he'd just heard. "It's seven in the morning. I saw a swing set in the back as we drove up. Are you telling me kids have left before seven am to go to school?"

"In some areas, kids are on the bus for nearly an hour to get to school," I said, remembering a report I'd seen on TV a while back about rural children having to travel long distances to reach their schools.

"Really?"

"Most of those areas are in farmlands, though," I admitted, poking a hole in my initial claim.

A noise like a crashing sound inside the house alerted us that someone was in there, so Alex knocked on the door once more and reached for his gun as he called out, "Mr. O'Malley? It's the police. Please open the door."

Just seconds later, the front door slowly opened and a man who looked almost exactly like Bruno Carter stood in front of us in a black silk bathrobe. He looked groggy, like he'd just rolled out of bed, but even disheveled, there was no mistaking how much he looked like Eliza Morrow's driver.

Alex held up his badge and said through the screen, "Mr. O'Malley, my name is Alex Montero and this is Poppy McGuire. We're from Sunset Ridge. We'd like to speak to you."

Gavin O'Malley shook his head as if to clear his mind and then scrubbed the last remnants of sleep from his face. "Now? You want to speak to me now? I don't even know where Sunset Ridge is. Are you sure you have the right person?"

"We're investigating the death of Samuel Morrow. We'd like to talk to you about your son and his mother."

As soon as the words left Alex's mouth, Gavin's eyes filled with a look of recognition. He may have been still sleepy, but that got his attention.

"Okay. Give me a minute to put some clothes on, okay?" he said before walking up the staircase in the center of the home and disappearing from sight.

When he was out of earshot, I turned to Alex and said, "Oh, my God! Did you see how similar he looks to Bruno? He's the spitting image, just about twenty years older than him. There's no way that guy could avoid admitting he was the father. Wow!"

"I have to admit they do look a lot alike. So much alike, I'd guess, that someone might confuse the father for the son and vice versa," Alex said quietly as he took out his notebook from his shirt pocket.

"Are you thinking that Sterling mistook the father for the son all those times he watched Eliza with Bruno?" I asked, my brain whirling at the concept of such a thing happening.

"I'm not ruling anything out. Either should you."

Alex's subtle dig about my propensity to jump to conclusions registered loud and clear. Nodding, I smiled at him. "I know. Don't get ahead of myself. I got it. You may not think I pay attention to how you do this, but I do."

"I didn't say that, Poppy. I just meant…"

Alex let his sentence remain unfinished, so I completed it for him. "You just meant that I shouldn't jump to conclusions, even though that's one of my more charming habits. Don't worry. I won't."

Just then, Gavin O'Malley came walking back down the stairs, now fully dressed in jeans, a navy blue polo shirt, and sneakers. His appearance had a quintessential suburbanite feel to it.

As he opened the screen door, he said, "I hope you don't mind if we take a little walk around the back. I don't want to wake my wife and kids. They have off from school today, so we got to sleep in a little this morning and we're going to take a drive to the state park for a picnic at lunchtime."

Alex nodded. "Lead the way. We can talk and walk at the same time, Mr. O'Malley."

I suspected the reason he didn't want to stand on the front porch and talk to us was because his neighbors might see a policeman at his house. However, the fact that we'd already told him we wanted to speak to him about his illegitimate son Bruno may have also played a big role in the reason he wanted to take us away from the house. I wondered which reason pressed more heavily on him.

The three of us walked around the house and into the backyard lined with a wooded area at the very rear. The trees had the full bloom of leaves, so in no time we'd left behind the eyes of his neighbors and family.

"So what's this about Eliza and Bruno? I don't know what she told you, but I'm not her son's father," Gavin said flatly in a tone I knew he had to be working to affect.

Alex and I stood looking at him in disbelief. Did he seriously intend on sticking with that claim? No DNA test was necessary to show he was Bruno Carter's father. All one had to do was look at the two of them. The only difference was Gavin was older and less muscular.

"Mr. O'Malley, the Sunset Ridge police department has no real interest in that, except as how it relates to Samuel Morrow's murder last Saturday. I will say, though, that you're going to have a hard time convincing people you're not Bruno Carter's father. Genes don't lie, and he's wearing yours all over."

Gavin opened his mouth to protest what Alex said, but even he saw no point in fighting the obvious. Sighing, he hung his head. "Fine. You're right. I guess there is no point in continuing to uphold the charade. I am the father of her child."

He looked up at us and continued, "Other than that, though, I have no connection whatsoever to Eliza or Bruno."

"Have you seen either one of them lately? Say in the past month or so?" Alex asked, his pen ready to jot down Gavin's answers in his notepad.

"No. Not in the past month. I admit, I have seen her a few times in the past few months. I did. But it wasn't anything bad like cheating."

I watched Gavin O'Malley answer Alex's question and tried to ascertain if he was lying about the cheating on his wife with Eliza. I couldn't tell for sure, but my gut said he was telling the truth. And what the private eye reported seeing bore that out.

"You mean like that picnic you and Eliza had during that heat wave we had in February?" Alex asked, surprising Gavin.

"How? Who told you?" he said excitedly and then paused before letting out a heavy sigh. "What am I asking for? We were sitting right out in the open by the fountain in Meridian Hill Park, for God's sake. Yes. That was me, but whoever you found that out from must have told you that it was nothing bad. That's if they told the truth."

"Again, Mr. O'Malley, we're not interested in whether you cheated on your wife or not. What we want to know is what you two were meeting about other than sex," Alex said as he wrote down in his notes REASON and then a question mark.

Gavin looked around, I suspected to make sure no one could hear what he was about to say, and then whispered, "She found me at the Caston Public Library and told me about Bruno. I told her I wanted nothing to do with that. I was just a kid when that happened. But she came around a few more times, and then he began to come around leaving notes in the books he brought back for her. I ignored them, but when she came up to me at the library at Georgetown, I agreed to talk to her. So we got together a few times and she showed me pictures of him when he was a baby. It was all a mistake, though, because she wanted more and I couldn't give her more."

The worry etched into his features as he spoke about Eliza and their son made me think he was afraid of them or what they'd do. I suspected she was the type of woman to threaten to tell a man's wife about his past, and by the way Gavin was talking, I thought he might be concerned she'd do that too.

Alex looked up from his notes and said, "So you met and told her you didn't want to be in Bruno's life. Is that right? Did she want anything else? Did she threaten you with anything from your shared past?"

"Yeah. I told her one day when we were at a coffee shop, and then the next thing I knew she was coming to see me at the library at school telling me Bruno needed my help and I was the only person who could help him. I put her off as long as I could, but she kept coming around. Last Saturday, she sat in the library for over five hours practically terrorizing me at my workplace. I refused to see her and stayed in the storeroom nearly the whole time."

Curious what Eliza could have been talking about, I asked, "Do you know what Bruno needed from you? What kind of help only you could give him?"

Was there some medical problem that only his father could help with?

Gavin shook his head. "No, and I didn't want to know. I never wanted her to keep the baby to begin with. I didn't want to parent a child with her. She knew that when she told me all those years ago that she was pregnant."

Alex continued to write down what Gavin said, so I

asked another question. "I get that you were young, but why did you say you didn't want to be a parent with her?"

My partner stopped writing and lifted his head, clearly interested in his answer to that question too. I understood not wanting a child when he was in his early twenties, but why not especially with Eliza?

We waited for him to give us his answer as I wondered was it her age? Or something else?

He winced like admitting what he had to say hurt in some way and then finally answered, "This is going to sound all wrong, but here it is. Eliza has always been manipulative. Well, at least with me she has. I was twenty-two, which was still young, but I knew I had no business being with a fifteen year old. She had a way of making me do things I didn't really want to do and then making me think it was my idea in the first place. I may have been stupid to be with her, but I knew what would happen if I stayed with her. So I broke it off and a few months later she told me she was pregnant. I didn't want to believe it was mine, but as you can see with Bruno, there's no doubt."

Alex and I looked at one another and then he asked, "Did she ever say anything about her marriage to Samuel Morrow? Did she say he knew that Bruno was her son and not just the man who drove her everywhere?"

Gavin frowned. "That poor guy. I can only imagine what he went through. I'm not surprised she went for a guy that much older than her. I mean, it's her type, but he had money, and that's all she ever wanted growing up. Money. I think that's why she was looking for a boyfriend so much older than she was at fifteen. She wanted to move up in the world. Not that she was dirt poor or anything because she wasn't. But she wasn't wealthy like a lot of the girls she saw at Georgetown, and she wanted to be like them."

The three of us stood there surrounded by trees and said nothing for a long moment until Alex asked the question that had to be asked. "Did she want money enough to kill for it?"

Gavin O'Malley remained silent, as if he needed to think about the question, and then answered, "I honestly don't know. Maybe she got tired of being married to Morrow and decided to kill him or have Bruno do it for her. I'll tell you this. She might not be capable of murder, but he might be. I have to go now. My wife and kids are going to be awake soon. I've told you all I know."

He hurried away into the house through the back door, slamming it shut in a sign I couldn't help but think was more about putting the past with Eliza and Bruno behind him than his talk with Alex and me.

"Well, that was interesting, don't you think?" I said as we walked to the squad car.

"I think that man is terrified of both Eliza and Bruno. I find that interesting," Alex said with a smirk.

"He should be. He thought he could leave both of them in the past like some meaningless choice he made about his shoes one year. He fathered a child, but he takes no responsibility whatsoever. That makes him a bad guy in my mind," I said as we reached the car.

Gavin O'Malley disgusted me. He was a coward who ran away from his child.

"But not our murderer," Alex said, leaning over the roof of the car.

"You don't have to remind me we aren't very far in this case. Everywhere we turn, it's all Eliza and Bruno, yet the two of them have airtight alibis."

Nodding, Alex tapped on the car's roof. "Well, if we can't poke holes in those alibis, then we need to start looking somewhere else for our killer. I want to go through that list of people Sterling gave us the other day. Maybe we missed someone."

As we got into the car, it was my turn to remind him of the fact that he'd checked that list twice already. "So the third time is going to be the charm? I don't think you missed anything. Everyone on that list either has an alibi or couldn't have done the crime by virtue of being on another continent."

"Then we need to figure out what we're missing."

Alex started the car and began to drive back down the cul-de-sac toward the main road into Columbia as I thought about everything we'd learned about this case. So far, we had Eliza and Bruno who looked like they may have had a motive to kill Samuel but couldn't have done it because they weren't anywhere near the jewelry store when it happened. We have a number of people Samuel had the private eye check out to dig dirt up on, but none of them could have done it either. What else was there?

Then it dawned on me. We hadn't found out how Jared could have known about the fact that my ring was the only item taken from the store.

"What about my ex? He seems to have known about my ring being stolen, even though the police didn't make it public. He knows something about the case he shouldn't, so maybe we should check him out?"

Alex turned to look at me and smiled. "I was

thinking the same thing. Let's head back to town and see what good old Jared knows about Samuel Morrow's murder."

Chapter Seventeen

ALEX PARKED THE car and headed into the police station, but I needed a dose of caffeine since I'd gotten up at the crack of dawn to go to Gavin O'Malley's with him. Six in the morning wasn't crazy early, I had to admit, but because I hadn't gotten up on time to make coffee, that trip to Columbia had to be done on just a single cup from some mini-mart just off the highway.

To say that I was feeling a bit sluggish was the understatement of the year.

No one stood in line when I got to The Grounds, and Gerald Branch waited behind the counter, an unusual sight for the patrons of the coffee shop. Usually his wife or one of their employees did the customer service part of the job while he spent his time in the back baking the pastries. Tall and thin, he didn't have a hair left on his head, a reality he always jokingly claimed had come about because of the woman he married. Unlike Pam, he said very little and often seemed standoffish, although I knew he was more shy than rude.

"Morning, Gerald! The usual, please. A French Roast the way I like it and a black coffee."

I looked behind at the display case behind him and

saw they had raspberry danishes again. A rarity at The Grounds, they were delicious, so when I saw them, I always made sure to grab a couple.

"Oh, and two raspberry danishes. I didn't realize you guys were bringing them back so soon, but then again, I guess since Christmas isn't really soon," I said as Gerald stood staring at me with a worried look in his eyes.

I'd gotten used to carrying the bulk of the conversation with him since he did tend to be on the quiet side, but this morning he looked upset. Had I said something to offend him?

"Is something wrong, Gerald?"

Sheepishly, he said, "I don't know how you take your French Roast, Poppy."

I chuckled, realizing that he likely wouldn't know since I didn't think he'd ever waited on me without his wife or one of the girls around. "Oh, I'm sorry. Four creams and four sugars."

He got to work making the coffees and getting my danish order together, and in just a minute, he handed me the cardboard cup carrier and a small bag with my breakfast. Strangely, though, he didn't let go of the bag and leaned in to speak to me.

"I heard what Jared said to you the other day when you two were sitting down at the table over there. He's trouble, Poppy. Stay away from him."

Looking around to see if anyone was nearby, I saw the coffee shop was still empty, so I asked, "Why?"

Not that I needed any excuse to stay away from my ex. Everything he'd done and said to me since that day he announced he'd changed his mind about marrying me and then ran off with another woman pretty much made me want to stay as far away as possible from Jared.

But the fact that Gerald had made the effort to say something to me about it made me curious.

"A few of the business owners in town have told me that he's trouble. He was working for Nate at the shoe store a while back and then just stopped showing up one day. Nate's too nice to say anything to him, so he's all nice in public, but privately, he's told me and a few other people who own businesses that Jared isn't someone we want to hire."

I didn't doubt a word Gerald said about my ex. It sounded like Jared through and through.

"Well, you guys don't have to worry about hiring him because Howard gave him a job at the newspaper. He's the new society page writer, and I suspect he'll soon be the writer handling the crime page and police blotter too," I said with more than a hint of disgust.

For one of the first times since I'd known Gerald Branch, he raised his voice and said, "That's what you did at the paper! Did they fire you? I'm telling you if they did, I'm going to cancel my subscription to *The Eagle*."

Startled by his outburst, which was so uncharacteristic of him, I immediately moved to calm him. "It's okay. I actually quit that job, so Jared can have it all. I hope he and Howard are very happy together."

Still upset, Gerald shook his head and frowned. "That Howard is a piece of work. Well, I have a feeling he's going to find out his new star reporter isn't very reliable. I expect to see blank spaces where your wonderful words used to be in the paper. They're going to sorely miss you, Poppy."

"Thanks, Gerald. I appreciate that. Have a good

one, and tell Pam I said hi."

He smiled. "I will. She and I decided to switch jobs today, so she's in the back making the baked goods while I take care of customers. You're just my second, but I think I'm doing pretty good, if I do say so myself."

I nodded in agreement and lifted what I'd bought as I said, "Coffee and danishes in hand and I'm leaving with a smile on my face. I'd say you're a hit!"

"Thanks, Poppy. Tell Alex we said hi and we can't wait until the wedding. Pam told me she saw him the other day and nearly talked his ear off about the whole thing. You know her. Have a good one!"

"You too!"

As I walked back across the street, I thought about how much Alex must have hated having to talk to Pam about the wedding. Everywhere we went, people in town wanted to discuss the details of our big day. At least when I was around, they could talk to me, but alone, Alex likely would have preferred to have every tooth in his head drilled without Novocain rather than chat about the wedding plans with anyone but me.

And the fact that he hadn't mentioned a word about it to me meant he'd hated it even more than I could imagine.

I opened the door to the police station, barely juggling the coffee carrier and the bag of danishes, and when I walked in I saw Alex, Derek, and Jared standing in the chief's office. As I drew closer to where they stood, I heard Derek tell him in no uncertain terms that he wanted to know how he knew about my ring being the only thing taken that day Samuel Morrow was murdered.

"This is unlawful persecution, Derek!" Jared

screeched. "You can't do this."

"Do what? Ask someone questions? Yeah, I can, dude. It's a big part of being a cop. I ask questions to find out the truth of who did what. Now I'm going to ask you again. How did you know that we found Poppy's ring missing from Samuel Morrow's shop the day of the murder?"

I stepped into the doorway of Derek's office and waited to hear Jared's answer.

But true to his nature, he acted like a mealy-mouthed worm and pointed at me standing there. "You're going to believe her word over mine? She has every reason to implicate me in this…in any crime! She still hates me for what I did to her! She told me just the other day."

Derek and Alex turned to look at me, and I saw in Alex's eyes that he'd had enough of Jared's nonsense. Slowly, he spun around to face him and said in a low voice full of contempt, "Whatever she feels about what you did has nothing to do with this case. The chief of police of this town asked you a question. Answer it. Now."

Jared's eyes grew wide with fear. He had every reason to be afraid. Alex had not a shred of respect for my ex, and nothing would make him happier than to arrest him on any charge he could and throw him into the Sunset Ridge jail for as long as legally possible. Actually, I had a feeling Alex would have preferred to simply smack him around, but since he was a police officer, better to take out his aggression lawfully and by the book.

Trembling in terror, Jared looked over at his friend. "Are you going to let them do this to me? We've been best buddies for years, for God's sake! You barely know him for like a fraction of that time."

And then he looked over at me and said, "And she's not even a cop. She's no one here."

I saw Alex's hand clench into a fist, but instead of cocking his arm back to hit Jared, he shot it out toward his neck and grabbed the collar of his shirt. Yanking him toward him so he wasn't even an inch away from my ex's face, he barked, "The only no one here is you! I've had just about all I'm going to take of you insulting my fiancée, so answer your friend's question before I start asking the questions and you end up spending the night in jail!"

Derek half-heartedly pulled him off Jared and pushed his friend down into a chair. "Stay there and don't open your mouth again until I speak to you."

Then he pushed Alex back toward where I stood in the doorway and said, "Let me handle this. I think you might be a little too close to taking his head off."

"For damn good reason, Derek. The guy's an ass and he thinks he can just insult Poppy wearing that smug look on his face. He's lucky I didn't deck him," Alex said, practically growling his anger.

Nodding, Derek couldn't do anything but admit his longtime friend was exactly that. An ass.

"I know. Why don't you two go down to your office and I'll find out what he knows. I'll come down in a few minutes."

Alex stood frozen to the spot, like he still wanted to let himself go and beat the snot out of Jared, so I tapped him on the arm and said sweetly, "Let's go to your office like Derek said."

He turned to look at me, and I saw the anger melt

away from his expression. "Okay. Let's go."

I slid my hand down his arm to weave my fingers through his, and he responded by squeezing them tightly. I had a feeling all that stood between my ex and Alex tattooing his face with his fist was the hold I had on him as we walked down the hall to his office.

Closing the door behind us, I placed Alex's coffee on his desk along with the bag of pastries. As he sat down, I said, "The Grounds had raspberry danishes, so I got us each one. Why don't we have a nice breakfast and enjoy a few moments of quiet together?"

Alex looked across the desk at me and gave me a tiny smile. "You don't have to talk to me like I'm some kind of crazy person, Poppy. I knew exactly what I was doing back there."

I took a sip of coffee while it dawned on me that Alex and Derek may have been playacting in his office. "Was that all pretend in there? Were you guys doing the good cop-bad cop routine to get Jared to tell you the truth?"

He shook his head and slid out a danish to hand to me. "No. That was real. If Derek wasn't there and I wasn't in uniform, I would have knocked him out."

"Oh. I thought for a moment there that it was all for show."

Taking a bite of raspberry danish, he remained silent while he enjoyed his breakfast. After he swallowed that piece, he seemed to have calmed down a bit more, thankfully.

"I hate how he goes around disrespecting you, Poppy. He knows if I do anything while I'm in uniform, I'll be suspended, and he knows that when I'm out of uniform I'm always with you, and you'll stop me from pounding him into the ground. But I want to."

I held up my hand and shook my head. "Oh, no. I won't stop you. I'd just stand by and let you go at it. Maybe I'd grab some popcorn and watch."

A slow smile lit up his face, and he rolled his eyes. "You're too funny. I think that's one of the reasons why I love you. Most women would have a problem with me wanting to beat the hell out of him."

"I like that you're in touch with your Cro-Magnon self. Plus, and let's be honest here, it would be pretty hypocritical of me to say your wanting to smack him around is bad since I'd love to do it myself. The guy practically left me at the altar, and every chance he gets, he reminds me of it. He's got at least a good beating coming from someone someday."

Alex took another bite from his danish and hummed. "Maybe instead of wanting to punch him I should thank him. If he hadn't been stupid and called off the wedding, you and I might not be together today."

"Let's not go overboard. I don't deny that good things happened after he and I broke up, but I wouldn't wish what he did to me on my worst enemy."

With a smile, my current fiancé said, "Okay. Beating him it is. I don't want to talk about him anymore, though. That guy irritates me."

"I'm all for that. Let's just enjoy the peace and quiet before Derek finds us and have our raspberry danishes courtesy of The Grounds. By the way, I heard that Pam caught you off guard and trapped you in a conversation about the wedding. Sorry I wasn't there to save you."

He grimaced at first but then shrugged. "It wasn't that bad. I think I'm sort of getting used to everyone in town feeling like they should know every detail about the wedding. I guess it's a testament to how close they feel to you."

I lifted my coffee cup to toast his newfound acceptance of our neighbors in Sunset Ridge. "Life in a small town. You can't beat it!"

While he had become better at tolerating the idiosyncrasies of the people around us, I wasn't sure Alex would ever really be a small town guy. That was okay, though. He had me, a small town girl, to show him the way.

Derek came in and sat down a few minutes later looking altogether too pleased with himself. I wasn't sure what he'd done, but if it involved roughing up his old friend, I wouldn't be objecting.

"Well, I asked him every different way I could and all he kept saying was he heard it somewhere but he doesn't know where."

"Then why do you look downright happy?" I asked, confused by the apparent discrepancy between his words and his expression.

"Because I finally let him know what I really think about everything he done. What he's pulled on you, how he's acted since he came back to town. Everything. And it felt damn good to tell him all that."

"Good for you! But that still doesn't get us any closer to figuring out who told him my ring was taken."

Derek's cheery mood seemed to dissipate before our eyes. Sagging in his chair, he gritted his teeth. "That's true. I guess I could go at him once more."

Alex shook his head and waved away the suggestion of interrogating Jared again. "I don't think he's our killer. I'm not even sure he's someone who knows anything. My guess is someone on the force told him in passing, not thinking it was a big deal. I'm going to go over that list the private eye gave us once more to see if there's anything I missed."

Derek stood and headed toward the door. "Then I have some officers to question because I don't want leaks on my police force. I'll let you know what I find."

My partners may have wanted to drop the Jared angle to this case, but I wasn't ready to just yet. He'd worked for a bunch of people in town who I suspected still spoke to him, so maybe one of them had heard something from him about where he heard about my ring.

"I think I'm going to talk to a few business owners in town, Alex. I still want to know how my ring fits into Samuel's murder. I'll be back in a little while."

He pushed back from his desk and stood up to leave. "Not alone you aren't. I'll check those names out later."

I stood up and stopped him with my hand against his chest. "Alex, I'm going to be right outside on Main Street, for God's sake. Nobody's going to do anything to me in broad daylight as I'm walking up the road. We just went through this the other day and I was fine. Sit down and do your checking. I'll be back in a couple minutes."

He looked down at me with concern in his dark eyes. "Poppy, Samuel Morrow was murdered in broad daylight. I don't want you in any danger because I didn't go with you. Plus, it's police business, so I should be there."

"Ah, but you forget that Derek made me a deputy on this case, so I am technically part of the police force. There you go. Now sit down and do your work. I'll be back before you know it."

Alex cupped my face in his hands and looked deeply into my eyes. "I'd never forgive myself if you got hurt, Poppy. You mean the world to me, and not just because the wedding can't happen if you're not there. I love you. Don't fight me on this."

I covered his hands with mine and shook my head. "Nobody's fighting you on anything, Alex. I'll be fine. I'm not going to get hurt walking up the street. I'm tougher than that, at least. You run down those names and check them out. I'll probably be back before you get done."

But nothing I said made him change his mind, so I brought out the big guns. The trust guns.

"Alex Montero, I'm going to be your wife in less than a month and you don't trust me enough to walk up the street and talk to a pharmacist, a shoe store owner, and a the man who's run the same hardware store for all my life and knows me since I was a little girl? You were fine with me walking up to Martin's Pharmacy the other day. What's different about today?"

Drawing his dark eyebrows in, he frowned and thought about my questions before answering, "You know I trust you. Don't say that. Of course I do. I just don't want to see you get hurt. What if the person who murdered Samuel took your ring on purpose because they wanted to get closer to you?"

I pulled back away and his hands slipped from my face. "I thought you didn't think that's what happened. Now you do?"

Alex took my hands in his and held them tightly. "I don't know. I thought we had a case against Eliza or Bruno or both, but their alibis check out and are air tight. Maybe Samuel sent the ring someplace for some reason we don't know, but so far we haven't been able to find that reason or where he sent it. Craig's called every jeweler in a hundred mile radius. He's even called pawn shops and nothing."

I tried to reassure him. "See? My ring being missing is probably just a coincidence."

"Fine. So maybe the ring has nothing to do with this case at all and someone killed him for some reason we haven't been able to figure out yet. He was wealthy, but so far, his wife and her son don't seem to be able to have done it. So maybe they hired someone. Or maybe one of those people on that list I have found out he was trying to dig up dirt on them and decided to put an end to it. I don't know, Poppy. All I do know is I don't want you to get hurt."

I brought his hands to my lips and kissed them, placing a kiss on the back of his left hand and then the right. "I'll be fine, Alex. I've never seen you so worried about me. Is this because of what happened with Jared back there in Derek's office?"

Alex hung his head and sighed. "I don't know. Maybe. I just can't bear to think of you getting hurt because I didn't go with you."

Unsure what had made him so worried about me, I wrapped my arms around him and pulled him close as I explained again I would be just blocks away on the same street he was on. "I promise I'll only go to a few stores and ask some questions. That's it. I just want to find out if Jared told any of them what he knew about my ring. I'll be back in mere minutes. I promise."

He lifted his head and looked down at me with that same concern in his eyes that hadn't left since I announced my plans to go do some investigating on my own. "If you're not back in fifteen minutes, I'm coming to find you."

"Fifteen minutes is fine. Just give me fifteen minutes plus the five it will take to walk there."

"Stop bargaining. Fifteen is it."

I smiled and kissed him softly on the lips. "It means the world to me that you trust me, Alex."

Cradling my face in his hands again, he pressed his forehead to mine and whispered, "You mean the world to me, Poppy. It isn't about trusting you. It's about not wanting you to be hurt."

"I won't be. See you in fifteen."

Hurrying out of the police station before Alex decided to change his mind and tag along with me, I began walking up Main Street first to speak to Mr. French at his hardware store. He'd been Jared's last employer, so perhaps he'd seen him and knew how he'd found out about my ring being missing.

Chapter Eighteen

TEN MINUTES LATER, I'd already used up most of my time and knew I wouldn't be back to the station as I'd promised, so I texted Alex to let him know.

> **Just finished talking with Mr. French. He's chatty like me, so it took longer than expected. Going to Martin's Pharmacy now.**

Alex immediately texted back.

> **Be careful. When you come out of French's, wave so I can see you.**

I couldn't decide if my future husband was adorable or just a worry wart. Whatever he was, I did as he wanted me to and waved my arms in a huge motion over my head so he could see me. As I turned around to walk into Martin's Pharmacy, he texted again.

> **I'll be waiting to see you wave after that store.**
>
> **People are going to think I'm a crazy person, Alex. LOL**
>
> **I don't care. I'll be waiting.**

This wasn't exactly the kind of show of trust I'd

hoped for, but regardless, I continued with my investigation and walked into the pharmacy to speak to Mr. Martin. I didn't know if Jared had worked for him since coming back to town, but his store stood between French's Hardware and Cardow's Shoes, so I figured why not. Maybe people gossiped to pharmacists like they did to bartenders.

A small crowd of five customers stood in front of the register, three women and two men talking about some new doctor that they heard was coming to town that summer. Mr. Martin stood up on his pharmacist perch talking as he filled prescriptions, telling them what he knew of this new person coming to Sunset Ridge.

While I loved local gossip as much as anyone, and a new female doctor coming to town actually interested me, what didn't was standing there waiting for all those customers to be checked out before I could ask Mr. Martin my questions. I could always stop back later after I spoke to Nate Cardow, so I quietly slipped out the front door.

Once on the sidewalk, I waved my arms in the air again for Alex, who quickly texted me a message.

Thank you. Did you find out anything?

I had to smile. My soon-to-be husband, police officer, and my very own worry wart actually did find some usefulness to my questioning people about what Jared may have told them about the ring.

So I sent back my own message.

No, but I love that you're interested. I'm going to Nate Cardow's store now. Need any shoelaces?

I could almost see Alex squint in confusion at that question and then roll his eyes. He didn't seem to get my sense of humor sometimes.

Every time I went into Nate's store, I remembered my mother bringing me there for new school shoes every August. Back then, Nate Sr. owned the store and the current owner, his son Nate Jr., would help out his father on weekends when he was home from a private school he went to until he graduated from high school. A little over ten years older than I, he never spoke to me or anyone else much before taking over his father's business a decade ago.

That quiet boy turned into a very talkative grown up, though, and every time Nate saw me, he always had something to say. I braced myself for a long conversation with him today but hoped that I'd be able to glean some information from him about where Jared had found out about my ring.

A broad grin spread across his face when he saw me come through the front door, and he stood up from his seat in a long row of brown leather chairs. "Poppy, I'm so happy to see you again. Why have you come to see me today? Do you need new shoes?"

I looked down at my black sandals and had to admit I could use new shoes for summer. But that would have to wait for another day. Today, I was here on business.

"Not today, Nate, but maybe before the wedding. I was hoping I could talk to you about something. Do you have a few minutes?"

No one but the two of us were in the store, so my question was more of a polite formality than anything else. He eagerly waved me over toward where he stood and patted the chair next to him.

His blue eyes lit up at my question, and he hurried to answer it. "For you, anytime. What can I help you with today, Poppy?"

I took a seat next to him and smiled at how kind he was to give me a few minutes of his time. "I really appreciate it, Nate. I wanted to talk to you about Jared Cooke. He used to work for you, right?"

Nate's joyful expression immediately darkened. Frowning, he nodded his head. "Yes, he did. I had no idea when I hired him that you and he had been engaged. When he told me what he did to you, I wanted to fire him right there on the spot. I didn't have to wait long to get rid of him, though. He was always late! I couldn't pay someone who couldn't be to work on time, so I fired him about two months ago in early March. Why do you want to talk about him?"

For a moment as he talked about Jared, I saw a flash of that sullen, almost angry teenage boy I used to see sometimes on weekends when he was home from that school he went to out of town. I didn't know what Jared had done to upset Nate so much, other than his tendency for being late, but it was clear he didn't like my ex at all.

"He does have a nasty habit of being late all the time. I guess it's good that he shows up for anything at all," I said, attempting to make a joke about how he'd broken up with me right before our wedding.

Shaking his head, Nate patted my arm in sympathy. "You deserve so much better than someone like him. You deserve a man who knows how to handle business."

I smiled, appreciating his efforts to be kind. "Thanks. I agree one hundred percent. But getting back to Jared, have you spoken to him since you let him go in March?"

"Oh, yes. You know how it is," he said, nodding as he spoke. "Even if you do hate someone with a passion in this town, it isn't like you can just go around letting everyone know about it. You know how life in a small town is, though, so I don't have to tell you. We all keep a nice face on, but inside, I think most people would be surprised to find what's going on in our heads."

"That's the truth. I can't tell you how many times I've had to put on a smile while that ex of mine was around when all I wanted to do was throw something at his head," I said with a chuckle.

My not-so-subtle way of saying I hated Jared made Nate chuckle too. "See? I knew you and I were more alike than it seemed. We go along on our way every day doing what's expected of us, but inside we know the truth. You're strong like me, Poppy. I like that."

"You have to be in this town, right? But guess what? I think Jared is finally going to get his now that he's writing the society page for *The Eagle*. Those ladies are going to eat him alive."

Instead of my comment making him smile, it seemed to upset Nate when he realized if Jared was writing the society articles, that meant I wouldn't be anymore. A dark look came over him and he grimaced. Nate seemed more upset than even I was when I heard the news that Jared was taking my society page work.

"That's your job. Why is he doing your job, Poppy?" he asked angrily.

"Howard gave him the assignment. It's no big deal, though, because I told him he could have all my assignments and then I quit. I expect the parts of the paper I used to contribute to will soon be full of nonsense, courtesy of Jared Cooke."

"That's not right. You shouldn't have been taken off that page of the paper. Your articles are always wonderful and so well written. I'm not going to buy another copy of *The Eagle* until they put you back on the paper."

I had a feeling Nate was angrier about my getting demoted than I had been, but he didn't have to be. Karma had a way of coming around and getting everyone, and I had a sneaking suspicion that Jared would be getting his any time now.

Smiling as I imagined the mess he'd make of the Founders' Day event write-up, I said to Nate, "It's okay. Maybe it was time to move on anyway. I'm getting married in a few weeks, so my life is going to be very busy until then. I'm trying to see it in the best possible light, to be honest."

My comments made the anger drain from his face, thankfully, but the look he gave me didn't make me feel any better than when he'd been so upset. I didn't know what I'd said to trouble him so, but now as he stared so intently at my face that I wondered if I had something on it, I became uncomfortable.

As awkward as I felt sitting there so close to him as he continued to fixate on me, I had to find out if he knew anything about where Jared had found out about my ring. "So have you spoken to Jared recently?"

Nate shook his head slowly. "Not really. On the street a few times we said hi, but that's it. Have the police found out who killed Samuel yet?"

"No. I'm working with them, but we haven't found out who the killer is yet. I want to as quickly as possible because Samuel was a good man. He didn't deserve what happened to him."

Leaning in until his face nearly touched my shoulder, Nate said in a low voice, "They say it's usually the significant other in most cases. Maybe his wife did it. She was much younger than he was, and now that he's gone, I'm sure the insurance check will be a hefty one."

Never before had Nate been this friendly with me. I didn't know why, but it felt strange. I usually listened to my gut, but part of me wondered if I wasn't just overreacting because of everything I'd been through lately.

This was Nate Cardow, the shoe store owner, after all.

I was just being silly. With all the wedding planning, Howard being a bigger jerk than usual, and the whole thing with Jared and quitting my job, it had been a difficult week.

The front door to the store opened just as all of this ran through my head, and thankfully, I didn't do anything awkward, like jumping up and walking over to the other side of the room. Two women walked in and began looking through the sandal display, so Nate excused himself and walked over to assist them.

Taking the opportunity to move, I stood up and walked toward the register on the other side of the store. Clearly, this was me overreacting. Nate had never been anything but nice since taking over the store from his father a decade ago. This was the guy who always supplied the candy for the kids at the town's Easter egg hunt. Ask anyone in Sunset Ridge and Nate's name routinely came up when anyone talked about the most wonderful people in town.

Get it together, Poppy. Clearly, that whole Jared thing is messing with you.

I knew what it was. What that idiot ex of mine said about me not being anyone compared to the police had rattled me, and now I wanted to prove to him and everyone else that I could truly help solve Samuel Morrow's murder. But I wasn't going to do that by seeing things in one of the town's favorite businessmen that simply weren't there.

The two female customers oooohed and ahhhhed over how great the sandals they'd tried on looked on their feet, and both women fawned over Nate like I'd seen people do for years. My gut had been all wrong. Nate Cardow was who he'd always been since he took over the store.

A nice guy everyone loved.

Disappointed in myself for letting my imagination get the best of me, I decided to wait until he finished helping the women before thanking him for being so nice to take the time to talk to me. It was the least I could do, even though he had no idea of the silly notions that had been going through my mind.

He and his happy customers walked up to the counter, chatting about the weather and how each woman couldn't wait to wear her new shoes. Nate smiled and complimented them on their taste in shoes as he took their money and then bagged up their purchases.

"Wear them in good health, ladies," he said with a chuckle.

"Oh, we will!" the two women said in unison before they walked out with their new shoes.

Just as he'd always been. God, I really needed to stop letting Jared get into my head. First his mention of Alex getting cold feet nearly sent me around the bend and made me think he was thinking of calling off our wedding and now I'd practically made Nate into a villain for no good reason whatsoever, other than wanting to prove that I could sniff out Samuel's killer as well as the police could. The sooner I admitted that Jared Cooke should never be taken seriously again the better I'd be.

Nate turned to face me once he'd finished arranging something under the counter. "Now what were we talking about?"

"Oh, it's okay. I need to go anyway. I just wanted to stay and say thank you for taking the time to chat with me. You're always so nice in that way, Nate."

"It's my pleasure, Poppy. Of all the people in this town, you've always been so kind to me and everyone here. I've never forgotten how you used to smile and try to talk to me when I was a teenager home from school my parents sent me to. I know I didn't say much, but I wanted to."

Now I felt like a complete and utter monster. The man remembered how I'd been nice to him when we were kids, for God's sake.

"Well, being a teenager can be rough. I recall those years weren't the easiest for me either."

He nodded, and I had the feeling he forced a smile for my benefit. "They were, but I never forgot you tried to be nice to me."

We stood there in silence for a moment since I didn't know what to say. I felt awkward because of my guilt at how I'd reacted to him just a few minutes before. I just hoped it wasn't written all over my face.

Nate motioned toward the stockroom door and asked, "Before you go, would you be able to help me with something? I don't know which shoes to display out of the styles I just got in, and I'd love if you could give me your expertise. It would only take a minute or two."

Hoping the universe would see I was trying to make up for being such a fool earlier, I eagerly agreed. "Sure! What do you need me to do?"

"Just come in the back and take a look at a few pairs. I haven't been able to decide which to go with. I promise it won't take long and it would be a huge help. You know, as a man, I never know if I'm really picking out the styles my female customers will want."

He walked toward the wooden door, and I followed him, happy to help. "No problem. You usually do a very good job of it, though, Nate. Those two customers who just left were definitely happy with what they found in your current display."

The stock room had two rows of tall shelves that reached all the way up to the ceiling on both sides of a long narrow aisle that led to an open area with an old wooden bench that I imagined Nate's father used to use when he fixed customers' shoes back when cobblers still existed. We walked toward it as I marveled at how many shoe boxes sat on the shelves and Nate apologized for the area being so dusty and cluttered.

"I really should clean it up," he said quietly as we reached the bench at the back of the stock room.

Nate extended his arm and offered me a seat in the single upholstered brown chair positioned next to the wooden bench. Unlike its fellow piece of furniture, the chair looked new. I suspected anyone having to sit for any length of time to do work there would want to have the newest and most comfortable chair they could.

"Please, have a seat. I'll get the boxes so you can take a look at what I'm thinking of."

As I got comfortable, Nate scurried away to get the

shoes he wanted me to see. "I was going to go with all sandals, but then I thought maybe a closed shoe would be a good option, even in summer," he said as he walked down one of the side aisles between the shelves behind me.

"That might be a good idea," I said, unsure if anything I could suggest would really be helpful.

This gesture was really more to make myself feel better after I'd been so foolish before.

He returned with four shoeboxes and leaned over my shoulder from behind me to place them on the bench. "Take a look and let me know what you think."

I looked back at him and smiled before turning my attention to the first white box. Lifting the lid, I saw it contained a pair of white sandals with leather straps and a yellow daisy flower added just above the area where the wearer's toes would be.

"They're very nice. I like these," I said as I pushed the box aside and focused on the second one, a larger brown box with black stripes.

Nate didn't say anything, so I opened the second box and saw a pair of black open-toed pumps with three inch heels. Nothing I would ever wear, but I had to admit they were gorgeous shoes.

Turning back to look at him, I smiled. "I bet lots of women would love these shoes no matter what time of year it is. Anyone who loves wearing high heels would go nuts for them. Are you thinking of putting these in but weren't sure because they aren't really summery?"

He nodded, and in a voice that sounded distracted, said, "I was."

As I replaced the lid on the box, I said, "You should. It's a nice contrast to the white sandals."

Nate didn't say anything in response. I heard a rustling sound behind me as I reached for the third box, and in seconds I felt a rope around my waist being tightened. Before I knew it, he had my hands tied behind me and was standing in front of me smiling like any of this was okay.

"Let me go! Why are you doing this? Untie me now, Nate!" I yelled, but I doubted anyone could hear me we were so far away from the front of the store.

Suddenly, he didn't seem to have any chatty banter to offer as he stood behind me. I heard a ripping sound, and then a second later duct tape covered my mouth.

I struggled against the hold of the ropes holding me firm to the chair and my hands behind me, sending pain shooting from my shoulder every time I tried to move. Crying out was no use since the tape over my mouth made sure no one could hear a thing I said.

And then Nate came around to stand in front of me and smiled as he held up a tiny black velvet box.

"I can't tell you how long I've wanted to give you this, Poppy."

He lifted the lid slowly as I looked in horror at the present he offered. I cried out for someone to help me, but no one heard me.

All I could hope for was Alex would get worried when I didn't appear outside on the sidewalk waving my arms for him to see I was okay so he'd know to come up to Nate's store.

But how would he ever find me back here in the storeroom before Nate did whatever horrible thing he had planned?

Chapter Nineteen

MY EYES FILLED with tears at what I saw in that little velvet box. I didn't need to ask him why he had it or how he'd gotten it. I instinctively knew, and that fact sickened me.

"I had planned this to go a lot smoother, but this will have to do," Nate said as he took my wedding band out of the box and held it up in front of his face to examine it.

"You killed him! How could you do that? Why?" I screamed from behind the duct tape.

Somehow, Nate understood what I said and began to explain why he did it. Or maybe he'd just been waiting for the chance to tell me his story.

He stared at my wedding band like it meant something special to him, but then his expression grew dark as he read the inscription that Alex and I had Samuel put inside. "You deserve to be with someone who doesn't put you in harm's way, Poppy. You should be at home right now."

I'd be at home, you murderous maniac, if you weren't holding me hostage!

"I have watched you for a long time. I don't think you knew that, but I did. You were one of the only people who was nice to me when I'd come home from that horrible place my parents sent me for all those years. I never forgot that, Poppy."

"Then why are you holding me here like this?" I asked, my words garbled from the tape over my lips.

He either didn't care to know what I said or just ignored it so he could speak the words he'd obviously waited some time to say to me. I listened to him as he spoke, horrified at the reality that poor Samuel Morrow had lost his life because Nate had harbored some sick fantasy about me all these years.

"Then when my father finally let me have this store, you would come in and you were that same sweet girl you'd always been all those years ago. Always a smile for people. I knew there was sadness behind that smile, though. I heard what that Jared did to you."

Nate stopped talking and shook his head. I watched as he swallowed hard before he continued with what he wanted to say.

"I want you to know that I did everything I could to make his life miserable every minute he worked for me. I did that for you."

I thought to myself, "Why didn't you tie him up instead of me then?" It wasn't right, but with every second that ticked by and no one came into the store, I began to get desperate.

"Then you began dating that cop and all I could think of was that you were going to be hurt. You were investigating crimes and solving cases with him, and all the while I worried something would happen to you. I was so worried about you that I watched your house most nights to be sure nobody hurt you."

That explained the movement I saw in the bushes

the other night and the footprint in the dirt. Nate had been there watching me, I realized in horror.

He stopped for a moment and then lifted my wedding band up in front of me. "Then you two got engaged. I saw you in Samuel's store picking out rings, and I knew you'd end up hurt."

Nate leaned down and brushed my hair away from my face. I closed my eyes, afraid of what he'd do next, but he simply finished and stood up again and continued with what he had to say.

"I just wanted to see the ring. That's all. Samuel had your ring out that morning and I only wanted to see it for a moment. But he wouldn't let me. He said I should come back here and do my work. He was never nice to me."

Lifting my chin, I shook my head back and forth and begged him to take the tape off my mouth. When he frowned and said no, I couldn't help but let the tears flow I'd been fighting since he tied my hands.

They rolled down my cheeks and into the tape, soaking it. Nate watched as I sobbed, looking uncomfortable and wincing with every moment he had to see me cry.

Nate reached out and stroked my cheek, making me sob even harder as the thought of what he planned to do to me settled into my brain.

"Don't cry, Poppy. Don't cry."

Finally, it got to be too much for him and he gently tore the tape from my skin. As he tossed it into the garbage beneath the bench, I stretched my lips to stop the pain of the stinging from where the tape had been stuck to my skin.

"There. See? You don't have to cry. You're safe with

me."

I looked at Nate Cardow in horror as he stood there in front of me holding the ring he'd killed for and talking to me like everything would be fine now. Turning away, I shut my eyes and uttered the truth I'd have to wrestle with for the rest of my life.

"You killed him for my ring. How could you do that?"

"He wouldn't let me see it!" Nate bellowed, making me jump in the chair. "I just wanted to see it. Why wouldn't he let me just see it? That's all he had to do."

I had nothing to say to that. What could be said? Nate Cardow had lost his mind, clearly. I didn't know why he'd fixated on me. Maybe because I'd been nice to him when he was a teenager. I had no idea.

All I knew was Samuel Morrow had been murdered in cold blood over my wedding band. How could I ever even look at that ring again knowing what happened?

"Poppy, you can't be unhappy. Finally, we can be together," Nate said in a soft voice that sounded like he was trying not to scare me.

It didn't work.

Turning to face him, I saw a look of hope in his eyes. How on earth could he think we could ever be together?

"I'm engaged, Nate. Alex and I are getting married next month. Alex and I are together."

His face grew dark, and he shook his head quickly and breathed hard in and out through his nose. "You can't be with him. You'll get hurt. He has a gun. You can get hurt by that gun. You can't be with him, Poppy."

"Nate, I won't get hurt. I promise. Alex would never hurt me. He wouldn't. If you care at all about me, you'll let me go so I can leave here and be happy. You do care for me, Nate, don't you? I've always been nice to you, haven't I?"

I spoke quickly, hoping to get all the words out before he stopped me or slapped another piece of tape over my mouth. He listened to me and heard every one of them, nodding as I got to the end of my questions.

"You've always been nice to me, Poppy. That's why I love you. You're sweet and you're kind and you like me. I can tell by the way you used to smile at me when you were a little girl that you liked me. Don't be angry at me, Poppy."

Shaking my head, I forced myself to smile. Nate was confusing my terror for anger, and I had a feeling I didn't want to see his reaction to real anger coming from me.

"I'm not angry, Nate, but you have me tied up and the ropes are hurting me. Can you untie me and then we can talk?" I asked with wide eyes as I looked up at him.

He seemed to think about it for a moment and then shook his head. "Not yet, but I promise, you won't always be tied up. I wouldn't do that to you, Poppy."

A noise coming from the front of the store made us both turn our attention toward the door of the stockroom. I strained to listen to what it was and heard a voice say, "Hello? Is anyone here?"

It was Alex's voice!

Frantic, I yelled, "Alex, I'm back here! He's got me back here!"

Before I could say anything else, Nate hurriedly ripped off another piece of duct tape and stuck it over my mouth, silencing me. I tried to speak again—to make any noise Alex might here—but my muffled sounds weren't loud enough to travel all the way to the front of the store.

Nate ran up to the door, and with one last glance back at me, walked out to talk to him like nothing at all strange was going on in the back room. With my heartbeat slamming in my ears, I listened as well as I could to what the two men were saying. Alex had to know something was wrong when I hadn't come out and waved on the sidewalk.

He had to know I was in trouble.

I heard his voice and knew he sensed something when he used his deep police voice to speak to Nate.

"Good afternoon, Mr. Cardow. I'm looking for Poppy. I saw her walk into this store a few minutes ago, but I didn't see her leave. Do you know where she is?"

"I'm back here!" I screamed through the tape, my words barely audible.

"I was busy with a customer, so she might have left then. Did you check the other stores nearby?" Nate answered in a shaky voice.

Alex said nothing for a long moment, and I knew he suspected something was wrong with this situation. I imagined he stood there at the counter looking around for evidence that I'd been there, but he'd find none.

My only chance was to keep yelling and hope he heard me. I inhaled a deep breath through my nose and began screaming the words, "I'm here" over and over until my throat became raw. My head pounded from the fear that no matter how much I yelled, he'd never hear me. My voice wouldn't carry because of the damn tape covering my mouth.

Panicked he might leave, I looked down at the chair and the bench nearby. If I could knock the chair into that bench, maybe that would make a loud enough noise for him to come back. In my terror, I somehow picked up the chair even with my hands tied behind my back and my body tied to the chair and began slamming the chair into the bench as hard as I could. Pain tore through my shoulders and down my arms as my body moved in ways it wasn't meant to, but each time I ran the chair into that wooden bench, the banging noise became louder and louder.

I coupled that sound with my screams of help over and over, and finally I saw the stockroom door open. With sweat pouring down into my eyes making it hard to see, I made out a figure but quickly realized it wasn't Alex but Nate.

My heart sank. Alex had left the store without checking the back room. He hadn't heard any of the sounds I'd tried so hard to make.

Defeated, I hung my head and began to cry. What would Nate do to me now?

"You shouldn't have made all that noise back here while I was out there talking to that police officer, Poppy," he said, actually scolding me for trying to save my own life.

I didn't respond. I didn't try to stop my tears either. After everything that had happened—Samuel's murder, my ring being the cause of it, Jared's taking my position at the paper and his taunting me into believing Alex might be getting cold feet—after all of that and now to be tied up and held hostage by the person who'd killed poor Samuel Morrow over my wedding band, I wanted to cry. I'd get out of that stockroom somehow, no matter what it took, but for that moment, I just wanted to cry.

Suddenly, I heard a noise on the wall next to me.

Someone was outside banging on the building. I looked up and saw Nate rushing toward an old wooden door that went out to the back of the store. Before he could get there, the door flew open and Alex rushed in with his gun drawn.

"Get down on the ground! Down on the ground!"

Nate spun on his heels and tried to run away, but Alex leaped forward on top of him and tackled him to the floor. Pinning his hands behind his back, he handcuffed him and said, "Nate Cardow, you're under arrest for kidnapping and anything else I can think to charge you with."

As he read him his rights, I took a deep breath and smiled behind the duct tape still covering my mouth. All my screaming and banging had worked. Alex has heard me and knew I was in trouble.

Alex had saved me.

He stood Nate up on his feet and called Derek on the radio for backup. "I'm up at Cardow's Shoe Store. Come around the back. Nate had Poppy tied up here. I've got him in cuffs, but I need you to take him."

Still holding onto Nate, Alex walked over to me and carefully removed the duct tape from my mouth. "Are you okay?" he asked in that tender voice I decided right then and there that I loved more than any other tone he ever used.

I nodded and stretched my lips to stop the stinging once again. "Yeah, I'm fine."

A second later, the ropes tying me to the chair and around my hands fell to the floor. I stood up and looked at Nate standing there in handcuffs.

"He killed Samuel over my ring. He admitted it to me," I told Alex, sad to admit the truth.

My partner looked at Nate and nodded. "Murder, theft, and kidnapping. You're going away for a long time."

He got no response, but Nate looked at me and said, "You were always so nice to me, Poppy. I just wanted you to see you were right for doing that. I wanted you to see I loved you."

I didn't know what to say to that. In Nate Cardow's twisted mind, everything he'd done had been to show me how much he cared for me. That love, as he called it, had caused the death of Samuel Morrow and led to him holding me hostage, tied up in his stockroom. I didn't know if I hated him for what he did or pitied him for what he thought was love.

Maybe what I felt was a combination of both.

Derek arrived to take Nate into custody, and I saw the shock on his face when he saw me standing next to the ropes on the chair. He didn't say anything but just yanked Nate out of the building and led him to the police car.

Alone, Alex pulled me into his arms and squeezed me tightly to him. He pressed a kiss to the top of my head and whispered, "Thank God you're all right. I wanted to kill him when I came through that door and saw you sitting there with that tape on your mouth tied up to that chair."

I leaned my cheek against his heart and heard it beating still so fast. "I'm okay. I don't think he ever wanted to hurt me. He just had some twisted fantasy that he loved me and thought we'd be together."

Tilting my head back, Alex looked down and I saw real fear in his eyes. "I don't know what I would have done if he'd…"

He didn't finish his thought and kissed me instead, cradling my face in his hands as he sweetly pressed his lips to mine. I knew as hard as this had been on me, it was hard on him too, maybe even worse because of what had happened to Helena. I didn't want him to live in terror that he'd lose me just because I wanted to fancy myself a cop. I couldn't do that anymore.

So it was time to let him know I'd made a decision.

Looking up at him, I smiled and straightened the collar on his uniform. "This was my last case, Alex."

I didn't know how I'd expected him to react, but seeing his dark eyebrows come in and an angry expression come over his face surprised me. Why wasn't he happy?

"You love doing this, Poppy. Don't let my worrying about you stop you from doing something that truly makes you happy. I'm a big boy. I'll handle it."

But I'd made up my mind. I had something different in mind for my future with him solving crimes.

"No, what happened here with Nate showed me that I want to do something else that involves working with you on cases. I've been thinking about it for a while, and I had planned to ask you how you felt about me doing it in addition to working with you. Now plans have just changed a bit."

A smile spread across his lips and lit up those dark brown eyes I loved so much. "Something else that will still involve working with me on police cases? What's that?"

"Let's go to The Grounds and you can buy me a much needed coffee. I'll tell you all about my idea there."

"After we go to the station first so I can get your

statement. You aren't just someone working on the case this time, Poppy. You're going to be the state's star witness because Nate confessed to you. But I promise after we get done, we'll head straight over to The Grounds."

I tugged him by the arm and we walked out into the beautiful sunny May day. Just as we reached the police car parked in front of Cardow's Shoe Store, Alex kissed me and opened my door for me.

"Tonight, we're going to Diamanti's too. I think it's time to celebrate."

Confused, I looked up at him as I sat down in the passenger seat. "What are we celebrating?"

Smiling, he said, "Whatever you're about to tell me over coffee."

I watched him walk around the car and couldn't help but love that even though he had no idea what I was about to tell him, he was enthusiastic about it. That man who'd threatened to shoot me that first night at his house had turned into my biggest fan.

It seemed only right. I'd been his since that first case.

He slid in behind the wheel, and I touched him on the arm. "What do you think about going to Diamanti's another night?"

"Sure. Whatever you want."

As he started the car, I sighed. "It's been a rough day. All I want to do is curl up in your arms tonight."

Alex turned to look at me and smiled. "I like the way you think. A night in it is."

Chapter Twenty

THE FIRST NOTES of the wedding march began to play, signaling it was time to leave the tiny wood paneled classroom at the church that doubled as my dressing room for the ceremony. I took one last look at my dress and makeup in the full length mirror propped up against a bookcase and looked back at my father who stood in the doorway.

"That's our cue," I said nervously.

"You look beautiful, honey. I wish your mother could see this day. She would have loved it," he said with a tear in his eye.

I looked at my reflection one more time and couldn't help but see my mother looking back at me. So much of her lived in me. I touched my cheek and smiled at the way she used to describe my skin as her words echoed in my head.

"You have a peaches and cream complexion, Poppy, just like me."

I took a deep breath and let it out slowly, trying to calm myself as wedding day jitters threatened to make me pass out. All the work over the months Alex and I had spent planning this day, and now it was here and I was a nervous wreck.

"I'm not sure my legs are going to hold me up, Dad. I'm shaking like a leaf," I said as I took hold of his hand and clung to him we walked out into the hallway.

He stopped at the doors that led into the church and clasped two hands around mine, covering it as he bent down to kiss me on the cheek. "Don't worry. I've got you, honey."

We stood there for a moment before the doors opened and the organist began playing the wedding march one more time for me to walk down the aisle to Alex. He stood waiting for me dressed in a black tux and looking more handsome than I'd ever seen him before. He was flanked by Derek in his matching tux, and on the other side of the aisle, Holly stood looking gorgeous in her pink bridesmaid's dress we'd searched so long to find.

My father whispered in my ear, "You ready, Elizabeth?"

I took a deep breath and turned to look at him. With a smile, I said, "I'm ready. I love you, Dad."

"I love you too, honey."

As my legs shook and my knees knocked, I kept my focus on Alex waiting for me at the altar and looking so calm. Maybe it was because he'd done this before, or maybe it was because he tended to be unflappable by his nature. Whatever the reason, he stood as a sign that once my father let go of my hand when we reached him, he'd be right by my side as always, his strength there for me to lean on.

After what felt like the longest walk of my life past all the townspeople who'd come to share in our big day, I turned to look at my father as he slowly released his hold on my arm. He kissed me, and turned to face the minister when he asked, "Who gives this woman away?"

With the pride he always had in me, he said, "I do," and guided me to Alex.

He reached down and took my hand in his as the minister began the ceremony. Looking at Alex, he said, "Alex and Poppy have written their own vows."

We turned to face one another, and the emotion of the day threatened to overwhelm me. But just the touch of Alex's hands holding mine let me know we were in this together. I listened as Alex began to say the words he'd composed to let the world know how much he loved me.

"Elizabeth McGuire…Poppy, you brought me out of the darkness I thought would be the rest of my life. You made me laugh and showed me I was meant for more than the life I'd accepted before you. You made me want to love again because of you. I love you and I promise to honor that love for the rest of my life. You brought joy and happiness back to my life, and I pledge to always do that for you."

His words took my breath away. Never a man to say much, he said everything I could ever want to hear.

As my eyes filled with tears, I smiled and mouthed I love you to him before reciting my vows to him.

"Alexander Montero…Alex, you're my strength when I think I can't go on, and I can't imagine living without you. You believed in me when few others did. You're my champion who cheers me on in your quiet way that makes me think I can conquer the world. You showed me I could trust again, and I love you so much for that. I pledge to never let a day go by without proving to you that you were right about me."

His smile told me I'd affected him with my vows just

as he'd affected me with his. Even though for us, we already felt married, we turned to face the minister so he could finish the ceremony.

Looking at Alex, he said, "Alex, do you take Elizabeth to be your partner in love and life? To have and to hold from this day forward, and to honor and cherish for as long as you both shall live?"

He glanced over at me and smiled. "I do."

Alex turned back toward Derek to get my new wedding ring we'd had made. He slid it on my finger as he repeated after the minister, "With this ring, I thee wed."

"And Elizabeth, do you take Alexander to be your partner in love and life? To have and to hold from this day forward, and to honor and cherish for as long as you both shall live?"

As confidently as I'd ever said any words before I my life, I said those two magic words to the man I loved. "I do."

I slid his wedding ring onto his finger and repeated the minister's words, "With this ring, I thee wed."

Smiling, the minister announced to the congregation behind us, "Then by the power vested in me by the state of Maryland, I pronounce you husband and wife. Alex, you may kiss your bride."

I turned to face him and wondered if I'd ever be happier than at that very moment. Taking me in his arms, Alex whispered, "Mrs. Montero, I think this is when we're supposed to kiss."

"Then let's not let all these people down."

And we kissed, right there in front of a church full of friends, family, and neighbors in our little town of Sunset Ridge amid their cheers and clapping.

We'd done it.

ALEX PRESSED A soft kiss onto the back of my hand as we sat alone at the last remaining table the caterers hadn't cleaned up yet. All the guests had eaten the wonderful reception dinner from Diamanti's and the gorgeous cake from Charming Bakery with the white frosting and pink and purple flowers everyone raved about. They'd drunk more than they probably should have and danced until their feet wouldn't let them dance another step.

The gossips had pronounced in turn as they congratulated us that our wedding had been perfect. My father beamed the entire time through the reception as his fellow Sunset Ridge citizens patted him on the back and his regulars made toasts to the father of the bride and their Poppy, the girl they'd known all their lives first as the curious child who spent too much time around the bar and then as the grown woman who stood behind the bar serving them and listening to their stories of the old days.

Derek and his date separated by the time dinner was served. I saw him talking to Holly, and after they danced, I thought I saw a sparkle in her eye as they continued to talk throughout the night. Derek may not have been the best choice as a rebound for her, but I liked seeing two people I cared about smiling again.

When the last of the guests said goodbye, Alex and I breathed a sigh of relief and relaxed after all the excitement of our big day.

Now just as our life together had started, we sat alone in the darkness of a warm spring night. I wasn't sneaking around the outside of his house, and he wasn't aiming a gun at my head, but just like that first night, it was just the two of us.

"Everyone looked like they had a great time, don't you think?" I asked as I leaned against his shoulder and played with the ends of his black bow tie that hung down against his white tuxedo shirt.

He nodded and kissed the top of my head. "Yeah, I think they did. I'd say we're well on our way to cementing a reputation for knowing how to throw a party, Mrs. Montero."

"We've got a couple hours before we have to leave for the airport. What do you want to do?" I asked, not really wanting to do anything but snuggle up with him right there.

But since the caterers probably wanted to finish their job and head home, I figured we should help them out. Even if it was our big day, that didn't mean they needed to work late.

Alex looked around and took a deep breath. "I want to hear all about this book you're writing. Which case of ours are you using again?"

I sat up and smiled. "Our first. The Geneva Woodward case. I'll be changing all the names of the people and places, so don't worry."

"What's the title?"

"The Eleventh Hour."

Confused, Alex narrowed his eyes and gave me that look he wore when he wasn't sure where I was going with something. "Why that title?"

Leaning in, I kissed my new husband on the lips and traced my fingertip along his jaw. "Because just when it looked like neither of us would ever find happiness, at the just the right time when we'd just about given up hope, fate brought us together at the eleventh hour."

"Well, then, I can't think of a better title."

I took his hand and tugged him up out of his chair. "We better go. Hawaii awaits, Mr. Montero."

Alex stood up straight and kissed me softly on the lips. "A whole week of nothing but you and me and a honeymoon suite we might not ever leave."

We walked away from the pavilion where the reception had been held toward his Mustang to go home, and I said, "A week of no work at all. No working as a Sunset Ridge police officer for you, and no writing for me. Here's to no interruptions for seven days straight."

"Derek better be careful. I might get used to kicking back and relaxing on the beach," Alex joked as we walked through the grass with the fireflies lighting our way.

But I knew better. For all he may have thought about Sunset Ridge being just a small town, my husband was as much a part of it as I was. It had its negatives, but in the end, Sunset Ridge was more than just a small town with too many busybodies.

It was our home. And in the book I'd begun writing the day after we solved Samuel Morrow's murder, it would be as big a character as my two main characters, the handsome yet enigmatic police officer and his amateur sleuth partner.

Alex stopped walking and pulled me into him. "Have I told you how much I love you in the past hour, Poppy McGuire Montero?"

I chuckled at the extension of my name with my married name. "That's a mouthful, don't you think?"

He kissed me, and pressing his forehead to mine, he

whispered, "I guess, but to me, you'll always be my Poppy."

And he would always be my Alex. And just like the minister said, we'd always be partners in life and in love.

Forever.

LOOK FOR THE PROJECT ARTEMIS SERIES FROM ANINA COLLINS AND NEW YORK TIMES BESTSELLING AUTHOR K.M. SCOTT COMING IN 2018!

About The Author

Anina Collins has always loved a good mystery. From Agatha Christie's Hercule Poirot to Sir Arthur Conan Doyle's famous detective Sherlock Holmes to Dan Brown's intrepid Professor Robert Langdon, she's spent some of her favorite reading times with mystery novels. When she's not writing her favorite mystery couple, she can be found watching entirely too much Supernatural and dreaming about the beach.

Visit Anina's Facebook page at facebook.com/Anina-Collins-429334270597293 for news about her books, along with giveaways and other fun stuff!

And sign up for her newsletter today for exclusive news first! Visit her website at aninacollins.com for more details.

Books by Anina Collins:

The Poppy McGuire Series
The Eleventh Hour (Poppy McGuire Mysteries #1)
After Hours (Poppy McGuire Mysteries #2)
Top of the Hour (Poppy McGuire Mysteries #3)
The Darkest Hour (Poppy McGuire Mysteries #4)
Happy Hour (Poppy McGuire Mysteries #5)
The Witching Hour (Poppy McGuire Mysteries #6)
The Finest Hour (Poppy McGuire Mysteries #7)

Project Artemis Series
In The Darkness
After The Storm
Behind The Scenes